MIXED BAG OF TRICKS
A SHORT STORY ANTHOLOGY

MIXED BAG OF TRICKS
A short story anthology

First published in the United States in 2023 by Murasaki Press LLC

Cover design by Stuart Bache

ISBN 978-1-7363835-6-8 (pbk)
ISBN 978-1-7363835-7-5 (e-book)

Interior layout by E.A. Williams; Editors: Britta Jensen, Nancy Knight, Heidi Asundi, Kara Stockinger, and E.A. Williams

Murasaki Press LLC
PO Box 152313
Austin, TX 78715
U.S.A.
murasakipress.com

CONTENTS

INTRODUCTION

The seeds for our anthology began in the midst of the pandemic. Our group of authors found each other learning more about the craft of writing over Zoom, either as part of a class with the Faber Academy, or from a women's writing group we had started when we met at The Writers League of Texas annual conference in 2018. While in person events were at a standstill, we all continued to write. I was deeply inspired by both of the communities of writers I had the pleasure to meet with these past three years. Their devotion and wanted voices galvanized my efforts to unite our artistic efforts with this anthology.

In those Zoom sessions, we shared our lives as well as our stories. We often laughed, got to know each other, and commiserated on how difficult it was during lockdown. During a time when we were physically separate, our artistic lives went beyond the transactional and a sisterhood of artists was formed.

As a result of that bonding between us as authors, this anthology of stories set out to do things a little differently than most anthologies: We began with the gestation phase, focusing on process. Almost all of the authors featured in this book were given a writing prompt by an author they were partnered up with. For example, my partner, E.A. Williams, gave me the prompt of writing in a setting that involved a cabin, a spooky atmosphere and the death of a grandparent. I gave her the complicated prompt of writing about a rainworld planet and two individuals trying to overcome their grief.

Each of us used the prompt from our partners to write a rough draft with the suggested prompt. After that initial draft or two, we met with each other to talk about the process of writing outside a familiar genre. Those conversations were absolute gold mines for learning more about each other's processes. I watched each author grow and develop stories that originally, we weren't entirely certain we felt confident writing.

We wanted to feel like we were collaborating from the start, instead of at the finishing point where most anthologies usually begin. There is nothing wrong with starting in the final granular phase of polishing, and there are reasons most anthologies have to operate from that place, but we wanted to experiment and attempt to stretch ourselves as writers. We also hoped to be cooperative instead of competitive in a world that often favors the opposite—to the detriment of the livelihood of our artists.

In addition, we wanted the profits from this project to benefit this spirit of cooperation, fostering craft and experimentation in other writers. As a result, sixty-percent of the profits of your purchase of this anthology benefits the Writer's League of Texas, a nonprofit which has been helping writers around the world, not just in the Lone Star State, expand and enhance their craft with their high-quality online and in-person programming.

We hope other authors will be inspired to be part of a cooperative and encouraging community of writers as they grow as artists, too. Thank you for being a part of our literary community by reading this book and continuing to support artists worldwide.

Britta Jensen
Managing Editor

IT WASN'T PARIS

By Ilene Haddad

September 2022

I wanted out of Texas. I wanted to see new landscapes, breathe new air. I wanted time—meaningful time—with my husband, Bill. After six years of hideous culture wars, three years of COVID, and two summers of convection oven temperatures, I wanted museums and cafes and yummy restaurants. I wanted to stroll elegant gardens and have my picture taken by magnificent monuments. I wanted Paris.

Bill and I were yearning for reconnection after months of barely seeing each other. His work often had him leaving before I was out of bed and arriving long after I was asleep. I'd wake in a morning haze as he bent over to give me a kiss. "Did you eat your breakfast? Did you let the dogs outside?" Then I'd pass out again.

I FELT a little lonely when I finally awoke to start my day. Bill had a life I wasn't part of, and I was jealous of his coworkers, whom he saw more often than his own wife. I endured the loneliness quietly until it sparked resentment about falling so far down Bill's list of priorities. I landed somewhere between making a bank deposit and checking email.

But my jealousy didn't outweigh the part of me that enjoyed the time alone. I didn't mind not having to make dinner or listen to TV shows that had alien theorists discussing abductions and ancient astronauts. (Yes, that's a thing.)

Most often, I went about my days in a silent home working as a freelance graphic designer, wistful for Bill's company. When he did have space in his schedule to sit with me for coffee before work, I treated that time as sacred. He treated it as a chance to eat Hot Pockets while sitting down.

I followed him into his office after our short breakfast. "My hard drive is slow. I think it's an easy fix for you," I said. "It's also dirty. Is there something you could spray on it?"

I assumed my near-constant yammering had something to do with Bill enacting a rule that when I wanted to interrupt him, I had to phrase it as a knock-knock joke. That didn't slow me down.

"Knock-knock," I said.

"Who's there?"

"Your wife."

"Your wife who?"

Our conversations were shallow and always brief.

"You wouldn't believe the report I'm designing—it's 48 pages long," I said.

"Okay."

"You know, it's really frustrating when you won't converse

with me like a normal human being."

"Who wants to be normal?

The man had a point.

Although Bill had a home office, he was hardly ever in it, so whenever he worked from home, I got excited like my dogs do when I return from the store—or the mailbox. Pint-sized pooches have memories like starlings that hurl themselves repeatedly against windows, and while my actions fell short of throwing myself against a pane of glass, the emotions were real. I'd had enough "me time." I needed some "we time."

In the summer of 2022, Bill would travel to South Korea for ten days to help install an art museum exhibition. I thought he could tack on some time at the end of his job for us to sightsee, but my ticket would've been prohibitively expensive, and since that didn't even include hotel, food, and other spending, we crossed that one off the list.

Next, we decided to meet halfway in Paris. I immersed myself in researching charming hotels and out-of-the-way restaurants. But it was hard—and very expensive—to put together that kind of vacation in a matter of days.

The anxiety I felt trying to organize this trip overwhelmed my desire to go. Worry that I wouldn't do a good enough job planning bored its way into my stomach, where mild nausea coated my innards. Mere butterflies weren't enough. No. Black grackles with angry yellow eyes flapped inside my belly. I felt alone, overwhelmed, and full of feathers.

We had five days to arrange our somewhat less-than-glamorous getaway, which would take place right after Bill returned from Korea. What about a road trip to the Grand Canyon?

Snorkeling in the Caribbean? Hiking in Colorado? But it was far too late to plan these vacations the way I wanted. All were given up due to cost, timing, or my husband's inability to plan ahead.

We settled on a road trip to New Mexico. This wasn't going to be the vacation I wanted, but it proved to be the one we needed most.

OUR PARTNERSHIP HAD GROWN strong over the years, but like an old car, we'd collected a few dings over time.

Bill and I never had the traditional seven-year itch. We had the "How hard is it to get divorced in Texas?" itch. But that was long ago. Now we loved each other easily, but the clear coat was fading and we were in desperate need of a rejuvenating paint job. It was time to knock out some dents and shine up the old beater.

Soon we'd have a bumper coated in desert dirt and dead insects, but inside the car we hoped for peace. We weren't going on vacation to repair our marriage. We were going to have it detailed.

THE TEMPERATURE SOARED to well over 100 degrees in Austin, so we were ready to split for cooler climes.

I asked if I could help drive, but Bill said my driving scared him, which nearly hurt my feelings until I realized he was right. I'd recently made a nice-sized scratch down the side of my new car while backing out of the driveway. I was a much better passenger than driver, so I just sat back and enjoyed the air conditioning as we took off into the already sweltering morning.

"Why is there a gun in the console?" I asked as I searched for a Starbucks napkin to wipe my nose.

"It's to keep us safe on the road in case we run into any ruffians."

He'd obviously seen *Fargo* too many times.

Bill grew up hunting. Deer, wild hogs, and other unfortunate wildlife hid, while he and his father and brothers stalked them. They also shot at targets and beer cans when critters were scarce. Guns were part of Bill's world.

I grew up sans guns and was very much anti-guns in my youth and young adulthood. Now I can accept people's desire to obtain their own food. Seems more humane than the life of grocery store meat.

A couple years ago, I found a folder of effects from Echo Hill, the summer camp I went to as a 10-year-old. Among the pictures of my fellow campers and letters from my parents, I came across something so humiliating I almost didn't tell Bill because it went against my anti-gun stance. Apparently, my shooting skills had earned me junior membership into the NRA. This was Texas, after all.

WE CROSSED MORE than half of the second-largest state in the nation with candy and chips as our main source of nourishment. Some of the drive passed in companionable silence—the strum of our white Camry on asphalt the only melody.

I used to think Bill was angry with me if he didn't engage while we were in the car. I got nervous when he was too quiet. Had I done something wrong? It took a long time to realize silence didn't have to mean there was a problem. I've spent many drives to Bill's childhood home in Waco, staring out the window between conversations, content listening to radio signals go in and out of range.

But any silences wouldn't last long on this trip. Like a post-menopausal four-year-old, I was never very successful at the silent game. And I had plenty of items to discuss during this drive. "No, we are not taking a two-hour detour to see the world's largest pistachio," for example.

"Isn't there an NPR station somewhere?" I asked, punching buttons on the radio as we cruised up Highway 87.

"You ain't from around here, are you?"

Billboards praising God and discouraging abortion dotted the highway as we slithered across the Bible's G-string (kind of like the Bible Belt, only grosser).

I scanned the distance for giant white swaths of hypnotizing, wind-driven turbines (aka: windmills) spinning slowly in the Texas heat. I was never close enough to discern whether the turbines were audible, but it soothed me to imagine a whooshing sound—like a light saber slicing through dense air.

The first leg of our journey took us to Carlsbad (about eight hours with stops), home to the fifteenth largest cave system in the United States. I am fascinated by caves. There's something so creepy/cool about them. I love caves so much, in fact, that I'm in the process of visiting all the ones in Central Texas with some girlfriends. But the enormous caverns of Carlsbad made those look like mere potholes by comparison.

The pungent smell of bat guano wafted from the cave's colossal entrance to a series of drippy chambers. Sulfuric acid eating away at limestone strata had formed captivating shapes. Enormous, 265-million-year-old melted ice cream cones and sizable popcorn deposits gave the rooms an almost carnivalesque ambience.

I'm not very claustrophobic, generally speaking, although I do remember exploring chalky caves in Israel where I had to crawl on my belly through parts of it. I forced myself through, desperately trying not to let a fear of small spaces set in.

Bill and I had squeezed through some tight spaces of our own. It was uncomfortable trying to ease back into each other's lives again, but it was the only way we could rediscover the pleasure of true connection.

On the other hand, Carlsbad's rooms were so large, it was almost possible to suffer from agoraphobia inside. Deep crevices we couldn't see all the way into loomed in the heavy darkness. We followed a softly lit path through room after room of stalactites, stalagmites, and the occasional pool of non-potable water.

The acoustics could carry voices a quarter mile down the pathway, so Bill and I whispered our wonder at the eerie subterranean landscape.

"I wish we had headlamps to see better," I said as quietly as I could.

"What?"

My voice rose ever so slightly. "I said, I wish we had headlamps."

"*What?*"

So much for cave whispering.

"We have some headlamps back home in the shed," he said.

He's very helpful like that.

Most shimmers back home came from our TV and laptop screens reflected in our glasses, with a couple of furry stalagmites nearby. That was how we spent what free time we had together.

It would've been nice to use those spelunking headlamps back in Austin—not because our house was so big (or dark) but because it would help us see around the next bend in our winding marriage. Like most couples, we've had our share of challenges. These challenges can be serious, like agreeing on how much money to save, or minor, like whose turn it is to let the dogs outside. (It's always my turn.)

"I need you to toast some waffles," he said one morning.

"You don't *need* me to do anything."

"I *want* waffles."

"Well, I want all the puppies of the world to unite so I can roll around on a continent-sized puppy raft."

"After making waffles?"

It turned out, a headlamp would just annoy me.

Digging down into the depths of my relationship with Bill used to be something I feared—a dark cave filled not with flailing bats but with the unknown. I was no longer afraid of caves, though. Our path was lit by our own hard work, moving forward in time and emotional maturity, thanks to a very patient therapist. We were in a better space, and I don't just mean in a cave—although being in a cave is pretty neat.

Bill and I used to argue on vacations. Once, while on a trip to Belgium, we had some transit concerns.

"Hurry, or we'll miss the train!" I shouted as we rushed across the station.

"We have plenty of time."

"But we need to figure out what the signs say in English!"

"No problem," he said.

We missed our train.

The worst was at airports. We disagreed on how early to get there. He thought an hour before our flight was enough; I thought four days. Compromise on that front took time.

Now we're more likely to be patient and work together to figure things out. Of course, it doesn't hurt that we have phones and apps to help us with transportation issues, but that's not the point.

Our calves tightened as we hiked the steep 1.25 miles to the bottom of the cave system, where we were greeted by the obligatory gift shop and snack counter. We purchased a touristy refrigerator magnet and bottles of water before taking an elevator back to the top.

We held hands all the way up, which was significant. We're not typically hand holders, but it seemed right at the time. If we had been teenagers, we might've snuck off to make out in a dark, damp corner, but all we could manage was this effortless grip.

It wasn't the trip I envisioned. We weren't gazing at the Eiffel Tower or wandering the Louvre, but we did find ourselves in a place we could make almost as enchanting.

Soon after visiting the caverns, we were on the road to our next destination, where the sunlight shone and the water was potable.

Definitely Not Paris

After stopping at the carnival of a town, Roswell (the perfect destination for my alien-obsessed husband), we were on the road again.

One of the benefits of having a spouse who travels for work is that I sometimes get to tag along. Bill's job has taken us everywhere from New York and Hawaii to Germany and Japan. But this time we were going on an actual vacation that didn't involve work.

In the past, when I didn't join him on his business travels, I felt forgotten and a little scared. I turned on every light in the house at night to feel safe. I didn't know how to load a gun, much less have the combination to the gun safe even if I did, so I used lighting as my main defense strategy against any potential criminals. Only the foolhardiest burglar would break into a house with all its lights on.

But I wasn't as impressed by Bill's guns as I was of his elastic skillset, which stretched from video production and technical design to art installations and artist calmer-downer. He even did sound and lighting for upscale weddings and often brought home flowered centerpieces for me. One of his business connections was how we wound up staying in a fancy cottage about 30 minutes from Santa Fe in the tiny town of Pecos.

At first, I was disappointed we weren't staying in Santa Fe itself but soon realized this was the perfect getaway for us. No work, no responsibilities, no Wi-Fi. So we drove down a snaky forest road to our final destination.

Tucked away by the Pecos River was a small house where we would be staying. Built by a local philanthropist, the split-level abode with its sloped red roof stood out among our thinly spaced neighbors' more traditional residences—all with red roofs, as the HOA (or whatever they call that in the middle of nowhere) required. It was like visiting a densely forested suburb without the playscapes and soccer moms.

Nearly all the other properties were vacant since it was a weekday, so we had the woods to ourselves. Thank God we also had a Dan.

Dan, the property's caretaker, was a lanky, gray-haired man

of about 70. He was warm, friendly, and a little quirky, as we found many people in the area to be.

"You'll have to excuse me, but I've had a couple of bourbons," he said, patting his lean belly.

I was smitten.

DAN FOLDED himself into a dusty pickup truck and led us across a scant wooden bridge to the place where we'd be staying for the next five days. A delicate mist blew through the pine trees that surrounded us as we unloaded our luggage.

When we opened the door to the cabin, billowing curtains unfurled from the entryway and waved in the wind like slate blue sails. I walked in first and was immediately swallowed up. I yanked at the curtains, feeling for a pull-string, but the further I wriggled between the wall and the drapery, the more consumed I became.

"Ilene, get back out here," Bill said.

"I'm trying!"

"Well, try harder. You're in the way."

I was a clumsy butterfly struggling to escape its chrysalis.

Bill blindly reached inside and dragged me back through the doorway by the hem of my shirt. Dan found the pull-string, and the drapes parted like theater curtains, revealing a glowing room filled with wide windows and a striking view of the mountainside.

Dan turned on the gas and stayed with us until the house warmed.

"Well, I think that's it. Time for you to put away your groceries and get this vacation started." He hiked up his pants and ran a hand over his five o'clock shadow. I wondered if he was going back to the bourbon and if he'd be willing to share.

He failed to notice we didn't have any groceries. I fingered the crinkly half bag of potato chips from the car. We figured there would be a grocery store in Pecos. We figured wrong. This wasn't Austin, where grocery stores were plentiful. This was a little town that didn't have the luxury of a supermarket. The next day our growling stomachs encouraged us to make the 45-minute trip to a store where we could have all the food we wanted, and we wanted a lot.

It was far too late to get groceries that night though, so we dined on chips and a couple of shrink-wrapped cookies pilfered from the fridge. I missed Dan.

Our deluxe lodging was situated in a river valley within a small community of bungalows in New Mexico's National Forest. People who've owned land there long enough fall under a grandfather clause and can stay within the forest's boundaries. It's a nice arrangement for folks looking to drop out of society. It would be a great place to cook meth.

But we weren't there for that. We wanted to reconnect with each other and invest in a new marriage model. Preferably one that was dent-free and freshly waxed.

At around 1,000 square feet, our "cabin" was more show-room than shelter. The bright kitchen, dining room, and den were on one level, filled with artifacts from trips our hosts had taken around the world. Wooden masks and figurines—undoubtedly not meant to be touched—stared down at us from high shelves.

I walked down five or six steps to two small bedrooms, also filled with art, including one piece made of straw on the floor of our room that looked like a giant pillow. I pressed on it gently to see if it would give. It gave. I stayed away from that piece of art the rest of our trip, lest I trip over it accidentally and break it into thousands of fragments. Not something I wished to explain to our generous hosts.

It was getting dark when my stomach bottomed out and a spiky chill glazed my spine. There were many reasons to be frightened: bears, mountain lions, aggressive chipmunks. Then there were the twin terrors of drowning in the river or encountering a murderous gang of woodsmen.

Being alone in this remote location put me on alert. Tiny goosebumps broke out on my forearms while I unpacked as fast as I could.

"Maybe you should bring your gun down here," I called from the bedroom.

Like I said earlier, I'm not a gun person. Since I didn't grow up with them, I'm not comfortable handling them (except at the range under Bill's tutelage, where I'm a pretty good shot), so I must've had a good reason for requesting one.

"How long do you think it would take our families to discover we had been murdered in our sleep out here?"

He came downstairs holding a gun-shaped pouch.

"We're surrounded by raw beauty, and *that's* what you think about?" He approached the bed where I was unpacking our clothes.

"You mean you don't?"

"My subconscious is more interested in sex and alien abductions."

"But how can you *not* worry about being murdered by a serial killer in the woods at night? It's how practically every good horror movie starts."

"We're in a remote resort for wealthy people. How much murdering do you think goes on around here?" he asked.

I chose not to argue with the man holding a gun.

THE AREA around us had been under forest fire alerts for weeks. Acres of trees just a few miles away were decimated by flames. Firefighters were still working to contain them when we arrived. Signs drawn by children thanking them for their brutal work peppered the roads. They were posted in businesses' windows and at the local diner. Fortunately, a series of showers before we arrived helped with containment and caused the Pecos River to run mightily.

Fire is a natural pattern of a forest's lifespan. These blazes are said to be a cycle of nature that allows the forest to cleanse itself before thriving even more than before.

"That's one way to renew something," I thought to myself. It wouldn't be long before baby trees poked up near the roaring river.

Fire.

Destruction.

Starting over.

WHITE NOISE

The expansive wooden deck at the back of our quarters was closed off by a waist-high sheet of heavy glass at the far end so as to see the surging Pecos River below. The river abutted the end of the property, where you could jump off into the cold, rushing creek should you have a death wish.

The larger bedroom had a huge window, which made it

seem as if we were floating above the spirited creek. The sound of churning water took some getting used to—like when I visit New York and have to adjust to a blanket of urban noises.

"I love New York," I'd said as we tried hailing a cab the night of our engagement, 24 years prior.

"What? I can't hear you."

"I said, 'I love New York!'"

"I'm glad you love your work, but we're on vacation now."

At first, I thought the river's wailing made a bawling baby sound serene. It was the sweet melody of a middle school's band practice, a whisper from an F-16 jet, a mammoth murmur of white noise. And soon that tone blossomed into a full-body sensation: a low-end buzz. The aural vibration eventually became as comforting as it had been jarring. My body hummed as I settled into our new environment.

The restorative water raged hard over slimy stones and rocky steps ranging in bulk from hefty snapping turtles to suit-case-sized boulders. Our own boulders included two elderly dogs and a 95-year-old house that was falling apart. Even larger rocks overshadowed us—like the years I suffered with chronic migraines. Between trips to the ER, I stumbled around the house or hid in the bedroom while Bill offered me soda and ice packs. The medication I once worshipped stopped being effective, and the constant pain led to a deep depression which affected us as much as the migraines did.

I stood with my coffee in hand, looking over the leap to the bubbly rapids below, wondering what class they were. I guessed a four based on no information whatsoever. There was some-thing alive in the river's lacy foam. I imagined myself trying to resist its perpetual surge, which lulled me to sleep every night, then woke me in the middle of dreams as a reminder of its ever-presence. A sneaky alarm clock on the fritz. Bill slept through it all.

Two bachelor bucks shedding velvet meandered by as I sipped my brew, reminding me that this wasn't really humans' land at all. It belonged to them. It belonged to this powerful river, which could sing you to sleep, take you on new adventures, or pull you under its frothy surface.

ANNIE! ANNIE! ARE YOU OKAY?

Six years earlier, I was in Hawaii. Eager to get into the water, I sprinted across the sand, flinging my flip-flops off along the way. A sea breeze blew through my net of tangled hair. Early sunshine warmed my shoulders. The beach was sparse and the ocean was mine.

I strapped on my neon yellow face mask and snorkel, stuffed my feet into a pair of flippers, then duck-walked into the cool foam. Bill was still asleep back at our bungalow.

Within minutes of entering the water, I was battling the chokehold of the Pacific's tide. I ignored the voice inside reminding me to relax into the water and swim parallel to shore in order to make it back to land—something I learned in CPR lessons I took as a teenager. Those same lessons had me asking a pallid, mostly featureless mannequin named Resusci Anne if she was OK. I'm not the person ol' Annie (or anyone else) wants in an emergency.

An invisible surge whipped my body around like a tornado, then slammed it onto the seabed. Tumbling across the ocean floor, I rose only long enough to gasp for air above the salty spray before being forced back down, dreading that I wouldn't take another breath. My ears filled with seawater. I was dragged under again and again. The unnerving rumble beneath the waves competed with the roar of the ocean above as I ruptured its surface.

Fear bled down my spine as I comprehended what was happening. I was fighting a rip tide. Under the water, my thoughts concentrated into one terrifying speculation. "This is it. This is how I die."

I grabbed for invisible objects while my head banged against the bottom. I dug my arms in hard and kicked like Michael Phelps. I gulped water and air. After several hour-long minutes (fifteen? twenty?), I finally hauled myself onto shore and dropped to my belly. I could hardly breathe.

The what-ifs were endless. What if I had smashed onto the nearby mountain of jagged lava? What if I were swept out to sea? Would Bill be accused of murder? Would I wind up on a true crime podcast?

I stood on wobbly legs, hands on knees. My snorkel dangled by my left ear. Snot and drool drizzled down my chin onto the wet sand as I coughed up the sickening water. Annie was definitely not okay.

That episode instilled in me an extreme reverence for water. The crushing Pecos River—the same one that snaked its way through western Texas and emptied into the Rio Grande—deserved respect.

I also learned that going it alone in the roughest waters isn't wise. I needed someone, like Bill, to help me through my toughest times.

Our marriage twisted and turned like the Pecos and was every bit as powerful. At one turn we could have been dragged under, but instead we floated peacefully on its surface. There were times boulders stood in our way, but we navigated around them, reaching out for each other in the cool waters of our life together.

I WAS USED to posting play-by-play photos online during most of my vacations—both to entertain and to remind myself of a wonderful trip when I skimmed through my social media feeds afterward. Normally, I reached for my phone every few minutes to post something interesting or funny we ran into during our explorations, but I (mostly) resisted the constant noise of the Internet while in New Mexico, which is important to note.

I'm an attention hog, so I love social media. It's like a big pen of slop, and I spend a lot of time rolling around in it—posting pictures of my dogs, reading comments, or commenting on other folks' posts. I also like writing dreadful haikus and reposting memes. I get a kick—and a shot of dopamine—from my online interactions. I think it's a great way to connect with friends, family, and even strangers. Bill feels like it's an invasion of privacy and a threat to our little pod. Perhaps we're both right. So, I tried restraining myself from being lured in by Facebook, Instagram, and other forms of social media. I wanted to be open to small moments with Bill.

"What are your thoughts on alien abductions?" he asked as we took our daily drive up to the small diner for breakfast in Pecos proper.

"I think they sound uncomfortable," I replied.

He raised an eyebrow. "Only if you get probed. Not everyone gets probed."

Alien probes notwithstanding, being off social media didn't

guarantee Bill and I would become closer, but I was more likely to notice if we did.

AFTER FORAGING for leftover food in the cabinets on our first night in Pecos, we left our little hideaway and drove 45 minutes to the nearest grocery store the next morning, and it was no Whole Foods. We strolled the near-empty aisles, grabbing dusty boxes of cookies, three frozen pizzas, and some candy bars. Bill's food pyramid. We stopped by the roadside to pick up juicy nectarines and plums so we wouldn't be constipated the entire week. We took our loot back down to the cabin and put one of the pizzas in the oven.

"At least you don't have to cook a real meal," Bill said.

"You mean one with vegetables?"

"We shall not mention that word while on vacation."

The next day, we set out for Santa Fe. The weather was cool in the valley but warmed as we made our way out of the lowland to within cell service range. We parked at a gas station and checked our email before continuing on. I didn't check social media, although I really wanted to.

First, we visited Meow Wolf, "a mind-bending, explorable art experience." Although billed as immersive art, Meow Wolf was more fun house than art installation, its kluge of 70 rooms connected by various means, including doorways, ladders, and slides. Spaces varied widely from a neon-striped hallways designed using forced perspective to a lighthouse-shaped photo booth.

We wound and climbed through dozens of alcoves, sharing our awe at the variety and immensity of the exhibition.

We crept down a dark hallway punctuated by dozens of

dead trees painted with colors that popped in the mysterious blacklight.

"Check this out—it's so cool!" I said.

"Very cool," he replied.

We visited a room painted with black-and-white cartoons covering every surface.

"Oh, I love this. How fun!"

"Very fun." (Bill has a way with words.)

Meow Wolf was a pleasant and satisfying way to deepen my connection with Bill. We actually *played* together. Plus, it scratched my itch to get out of Texas.

Santa Fe is known for its art: the Georgia O'Keefe Museum, International Gallery of Folk Art, and dozens more. But the day we arrived, the galleries were closed. I guessed we weren't the only ones on vacation. I was disappointed. Somehow this re-inflamed that gremlin inside who was angry about not going to Paris.

"I'll bet Versailles is open."

"What?"

"Never mind."

But being mad wouldn't open the galleries, so before long, we zigzagged back down to our little river valley for some cookies and shut-eye.

THE REST of our trip was spent napping in our floating bed and roaming above the thundering Pecos.

"Be careful," Bill said as I balanced on a rock and held onto a young pine to get a better view of the river.

"I'm fine!"

"You don't look fine," he said from a yard away.

I danced a little jig to show him how fine I was, then quickly realized how fine I was. A literal tree-hugger, I embraced that bendy sapling like a long-lost friend, while my *best* friend looked on with worry for my safety. Later, I would embrace this less-bendy pal of mine, but in a safer location.

ON OUR LAST day in Pecos, Bill and I loaded up the car and prepared to leave. We were closer than we'd been in months. Bill's chronic, stress-induced neck crook was smoothed out, if only temporarily, and he seemed mellower than I'd seen him in months. We needed this time to focus on our relationship and connect on a deeper level, and in so doing, we found each other again.

Bill would soon be heading back to his savage work schedule, and I worried that I'd lose him to his job once more. I hoped he would bring home a little tranquility and remember what it was like to connect more fully with me and perhaps even with himself. I also hoped I wouldn't feel as lonely after all this togetherness, and maybe we would make time for each other in the days, weeks, and months to come.

"Hey babe," he said as we headed off on our long drive home.

"What's up?"

"Have I told you recently that I love you?"

"Nope."

"Well, I do."

That old beater was beginning to shine.

AWARD-WINNING essayist Ilene Haddad is a graphic designer, cartoonist, and writer from Austin, Texas. Her work has appeared in *The New York Times,* Austin's NPR station, *Next Avenue, Erma Bombeck Writers' Workshop,* and other publications. She is an active member of the Writers' League of Texas and was presented with the Women in Communications Creative Initiative Award for founding BlogathonATX, a central Texas blogging conference. Ilene lives with her husband, Bill, a lazy lapdog named Harry, and Dexter, the ghost of poodles past—all of whom appear in her current project, a collection of illustrated personal essays.

Website: casaweenie.com
Instagram: @casaweenie

CLIMBING

By Kara Stockinger

"Don't fall."

The silence that followed Jak's low-voiced warning was more telling than his words. Synth kids had entered the school lounge. I clung midway up the wall, nerves pulsing with sensitivity, as if a heat beam had landed on me. Whispers rustled below me. I should get down before they called a teacher.

Instead, I closed my eyes, focusing on the cool, smooth surface beneath my fingers and toes. This wall begged to be climbed—a high stretch of gleaming iridescent blue, with odd-spaced grooves just deep enough to grip. Opening my eyes, I stretched up my hand for the next notch.

I heard Jak's impatient exhale and glanced down at the top of his sandy-haired head. I'd roped him into playing lookout. He stood, leaning against the wall, flipping images on his wrist-vid.

Sorry, Jak. I was tired of skulking around this school like we'd broken in.

I pulled myself up another body length. Movement caught my attention, a flutter of white hair. A synth girl was scaling the wall, climbing with spider ease until she drew alongside me. I felt the cold weight of her eyes but refused to meet them.

"Hey, boy." The girl's voice was a soft scratch. "What is this game?"

I looked at her. I couldn't help it. None of them had spoken to me before.

Her grin slashed through an angular face, making her expression seem more impishly smug. Oria Gajena. *The crazy one.* Rumors claimed her father was one of The Fifty, the military unit that had slaughtered one another in a demented frenzy —the final spark that had ignited riots protesting the bioengineering system. True or not, the glittering of her pale eyes made her look like she might snap at any second and take a chunk out of someone with her teeth. Someone like me, for example.

Realizing I was staring, I jerked my gaze away. The synths were itching for one of us to cross the line they'd drawn.

Pride kept me straight-lining up the wall, not resting, not rushing. Someday, I might need this skill to survive. It was just a joke to the synth girl. She mirrored each move, eliciting hisses of laughter from the others—two, I gauged by the direction of the voices. I narrowed my world down to the shifts of my grip, to the challenge of finding the right notch to propel me upward.

The synth arced up her hand, placed it with exaggerated deliberateness millimeters from mine. My hand slipped. I barely managed to cling on with the other, my toes digging into their notches as if they could burrow into the unyielding material.

"Bram," Jak called, voice ironed calm. *Come down, idiot,* he meant.

Oria craned her neck, peering at me. "You do realize this isn't an exercise installation?"

"Don't fall, thick-neck," a male voice nipped from below. I placed it. Red—our name for him—vermilion hair, shock-white skin. Dramatic contrasts had been in vogue during this synth batch's design year.

I couldn't help but glance down. I was three-quarters of the way up, a good fifteen-foot drop. Red stood below with a black-haired boy. They gawked, begrudgingly compelled by my low-class act.

The thought that the synth girl might reach the top before me stung deep. Setting my jaw, I pushed upward. My fingertips slid over the lip of a notch. I dug in with my nails and clawed my way to a more secure purchase. One notch, two. My body trembled with fatigue, screaming for me to give up. I didn't.

I felt Oria watching as she matched me, like I was a bug under magnification. "Stubborn," she muttered then surged upward, nimbling her way to the top in seconds.

My teeth snapped together hard enough to hurt.

She hovered there, her hair lit green by the holo-slogan projected under the rafter: *Revner colonists stand together!* She watched me absorb her superior position. Tilting her head as if in inquiry, she pushed off the wall—let go.

My stomach swooped, and I almost lost my grip. She landed on the floor with liquid grace. Lifting her face toward me, she asked, "Were you worried?"

I sensed Red's gaze ice over and jerked my focus back to the wall. My hands shook, growing slick with sweat. I was high—too high. Time to stop being an idiot.

My knuckles throbbed, my strength fraying as I scrabbled

my way down. Two notches. A body length. Another. Then my limbs seemed to forget their task. One instant I was holding on, the next I was skidding down the wall. I landed hard on my ass, pain zapping up my tailbone.

The soft resin flooring had buffered my fall or I'd have broken something. Until two weeks ago, this had been a synth-only school. Now the floor was scarred and streaked by our cheap-soled shoes.

The synth boys started clapping. "Let's hope it doesn't urinate on the floor next," the black-haired one said.

Waiting out the pain, I didn't try to rise but slid around to face the room. Jak edged to my side, his raw-boned face ruddy with anger. Lately, the breezy sarcasm he'd met the world with had condensed into something harder. He wouldn't help me up with them watching.

My scalp prickled as I spotted Oria, crouched close. "That was fun. Let's do it again sometime." Her voice was low and smoky for a girl's. This close, I could see the eerie smoothness of her skin, like she had no pores to sweat from. There was something discordant about her design, too sharp-edged. And her golden-brown skin contrasted oddly with frosty white hair and pale, silvery eyes.

Before this school term, I'd never been this close to synth kids. We'd been at different schools. In different neighborhoods. Of different strata.

Red sniffed to alertness. "What are you looking at, thick-neck?"

I glanced at Jak, whose mouth had thinned. Naturals were all "thick-necks" to them: dumb, ugly clods. Synths were sleek—pure optimized muscle. I envied their lean strength, but not because I thought it was pretty.

Jak's hitched breath alerted me an instant before a force slammed me onto my back. My head cracked against the wall. Red's rage-splotched face hovered over me. He pinned my legs with his knees, my shoulders with his fists.

My eyes rolled to Jak—not a plea for help, but a warning as his body bunched, priming to help me. *Don't!*

"Keep your dirty eyes to yourself." Red pressed harder.

This synth wasn't angry about Oria, only pissed because we'd encroached on his air.

"You think coming here makes you our equal, thick-neck? Those limp-kneed officials can toss whatever pity prizes they want. Doesn't change the fact that you're all unplanned mongrels." His voice vibrated with anger, like he wanted to shake the whole world apart with it. My fear shrank to a hard kernel; beneath the hate in his eyes, I saw *his* fear. The privileges synths once took for granted had been whittled away. Red was scared of where they'd bottom out.

I studied him, feeling disconnected from my danger. Something twitched under his bland symmetry. Inbred, maybe. Now that the lid on the synth system had been pried open, dirt was pouring out. Some designers had swindled naturals who could afford "planning," taking the money but basing the kids on their own genetic material. Twisted narcissism.

Every muscle in my face tightened as Jak surged forward, but the black-haired synth blocked him with a shove. We couldn't call for help. Justice might have liberated city folk, but its slow crawl from the capital hadn't reached us here in the Fells.

Red rested the pad of his hand over my throat where my pulse raced. His eyes slitted as if he imagined crushing my windpipe. "You don't get to look at her or—"

Impact drove the words from his mouth. Red flew off me onto the ground. I lifted my head, terrified I'd find Jak standing there. I stared stupidly at Oria's furious face instead. She glared at Red, who sprang to his feet. He looked as shocked as I felt.

"I don't need your protection. Certainly not from *this*." She flung a hand toward me.

The fury spots on Red's cheeks strobed. Then he inched back, as if afraid of her. "We need to establish boundaries with these cave dwellers."

Typical synth, so confident that he lived by different standards.

Oria bent over me, her eyes settling on my throat. Twitching with the urge to crawl away, I noticed a birthmark under her jawline. Synth designers labeled their works. Hers stunned me, a red sun. *Moncreed*. Their specialty had been designing soldiers, *all male*, or so the news tabs claimed.

Her gaze clicked to mine. "I think this one has set his own boundaries, but they're well inside ours." She straightened, curling her lip at Red. "This should be beneath you."

His eyelids flared as he turned from her. He shot me a look of pure venom before stalking away. The other synth boy followed, a smirk pinned to his face.

I pushed to my feet, feeling like my bones had been shaken loose and reassembled. My head throbbed.

Jak dusted off his shirt as if flinging off the synth's touch. I met his eyes—storm gray, dead serious. "What the hells, Bram?" he mouthed.

I shook my head. I couldn't guess Oria's game, but making two synth enemies in as many weeks didn't promise a smooth close to my school career.

· · ·

"I'M THE HOT HEAD, REMEMBER?" Jak said through the stim-stick he was chewing. Then he leapt off the auto-tram.

I jumped after him, and the tram wobbled away on its circuit around town. We started down the road home, avoiding the cracks and pits in the weathered pavement by rote. An autumn wind crackled through the scrubby trees lining our path.

"It wasn't that," I muttered.

"No?" Jak cocked a brow. "I think the crazy one likes you. Or she wants to drink your blood."

"Hilarious."

Jak raked a hand through his close-clipped hair—still adjusting to the cut. "I've caught her staring at you before."

I'd noticed her staring, too. Oria stood out, moving with serpent smoothness, while the others moved like they resented the ground for touching their feet. Not that we interacted much. Laws no longer segregated us, but genetics did the job almost as well. All synth kids were in the accelerated program. The few of us who could keep up with them chose not to.

"Hey, curly boy!" a familiar voice shouted from behind us.

Jak's older brother Nalen was the only one who called me that. I turned to see him leap from the bed of an approaching wheeled truck. Two guys I knew were smuggler links occupied the cab. They gave Jak and me a squinty perusal before driving off, over-rotating the tires to punctuate their exit with a dust plume.

"Don't listen to his shit," Jak whispered to me, greeting his brother with a frown.

Nalen looked like a puffed-up version of Jak, heavy set with fleshier features. He gave me his game-running grin. "How you doing at your new lab-toy school?"

I shrugged. "As you'd expect." Jak and I had trailed after Nalen like a forked tail when we were little, chasing glory in the trouble he found.

"You give any thought to hunting moondrops for me?" Moondrops, local slang for the rare, prized—and illegal— euphoria fungus.

"Shut it, Nalen," Jak snapped. "Bram isn't crazy enough to buy into your scheme."

Nalen ignored him, slinging an arm around my shoulders. I smelled the tang of reefer and sweat. "Nothing around here can match the take."

"Then you do it," Jak said.

Nalen gave my shoulder a squeeze. "Only a slap on the wrist if you're caught."

I was underaged, but that didn't mean an arrest for black-market dealing wouldn't cloud my future.

"You were always the best scaler." Nalen kept the gleam of his persuasion on me. "Like a curly-headed spider."

I thought of Oria and frowned.

This wasn't the first time I'd heard Nalen's pitch. I'd consid-ered it—too often. I rubbed my thigh where I bore a scar from the last time I'd let the idea tempt me and secretly made a run to test my strength.

"If your *spiders* weren't getting squished, you wouldn't bother with Bram." Anger crept up Jak's neck.

The entrance to our portable park spared me from weighing in. From beside the 2D sign ("*Polly's Portables: customizable!*") Mr. Rideki flipped a hand in greeting. His bulk overflowed the faded blue plastic chair that served as his guard post. No one paid him to sit there; he was self-appointed.

"Evening, Mr. R.," Nalen said with a grin.

"You used to be such a good boy." Mr. Rideki gave Nalen a pucker face.

Not true. Nalen was never a good boy.

"See you all," I said, ducking from under Nalen's arm.

Jak fisted his brother's shirt and steered him down the weedy trail that led to their two-unit. Foot-tramped paths hodgepodged around all the portables. I took the one leading to my family's four-unit. Its sides were gray-streaked from recent particle rains. Gramp had said he'd take care of it. Sighing, I palmed my way through the door.

"Bramalam!"

Mom liked to greet me as if she was renaming me, something different every time. It was funny when I was ten.

She stood at the counter over a scattering of small bins, her plait of hair a coarse rope down her back. Mom's latest part-time job was threading beads for bracelets. A fad for "handmade" had sparked a mini-market for the things. It wouldn't last.

"Come on, Bramy." She laughed at my expression.

"I'm seventeen. Save it for Cam."

My little brother looked up from his perch at the table, drawing on the embedded-vid—a copy of me at that age with his tight-kinked hair, oversized knob of a nose, and medium-beige skin sunbaked darker. He flicked up a thumb in greeting, once the secret sign of the Movement. Six-year-old Cam didn't know much about that, but he thought it looked cool.

"You need a haircut." Mom tugged one of my dark curls, anxious thoughts churning behind her eyes.

"I'm growing it out." We needed to stock the food processor more than I needed a haircut—even if I did look like I was tempting rodents to nest on my head.

"Any word on that opportunity?" Mom's voice was too

breathy to carry the casual tone she wanted.

I'd told her I might get a night shift fish-packing. A lie. Even crappy shifts were rare gems these days, but her anxiety was killing me. "Not yet. Might go tonight, follow up."

Or something.

Mom's eyes met mine. I could read the script running through her mind—*don't go, you need to rest, focus on school*—but the words didn't come out. Even an optimist like Mom knew we'd passed beyond that.

"Okay." She blinked down at her bowl.

My eyes were like my mother's, dark and deep-set. An ex had called them "melty." Maybe that was what had attracted Oria Gajena's attention—I looked like easy prey.

Those synths weren't keeping me from graduating. I had to believe progress would creep its way to the Fells. Maybe my resemblance to my mother went beyond our eyes. Maybe I was an optimist, too. I glanced at Mom's wall hologram of the Movement's leader. Gramp refused to eat "with that ineffective flitwit" staring down at him. Mom refused to remove it—thereby granting us peace during meals.

I heard Gramp's raspy cackle through the curtain leading to the leisure unit, which was basically his room, since he slept there.

"Gramp lit again?" I asked Mom, low.

She shook her head. Not a denial. "He spent his pension this month fixing his vid."

That wouldn't stop him from begging for credits to feed his habit. I longed to shove him out the door. Things were hard enough.

Hence the need for beading. Or data voiceover, or babysitting—or any of the other things Mom did to make ends meet.

She'd had a decent job with Food Innovations, until the new restrictions shut it down. No more bioengineered *anything*. That included the moondrops Nalen dealt in; once labeled a safe alternative to pain and psych meds, now labeled contraband.

I sat across from Cam and waved up my tab on the table-vid. Revner Colony needed alternatives. There must be something we could farm now, some *natural* things that off-worlders were itching to buy. Something that would grow without proper soil. In heavy water. Through unpredictable weather. I sighed and rubbed my eyes.

"Tired?"

I looked up to find Mom watching. "Just thinking."

"Want to talk about it?"

"Just homework."

"Things at school okay?"

"Sure." I didn't want her to press me. I knew where it would lead.

She scented trouble in my manner. "And the, um, designed children are treating you well?"

"What?! Of course, they aren't," Gramp called through the curtain. He had an uncanny ability to sniff out "starry nonsense," even when zoned out on vid-dramas. "This is the dumbest idea those Counsel flakes have come up with yet. It's like putting cats and dogs together and asking no one to bark."

I gave Mom credit. She ignored Gramp's first salvo.

"We won't be making friends," I said. "But the school's ag-science program is cool."

My attempt to reroute Mom failed miserably. "I'm sure there will be an adjustment period, but you must remember to judge every person on his own merit."

"That's what we *used to* do," Gramp interjected. He bought the old line that synths made better leaders, worked harder and smarter, deserved social elevation.

Mom flared up, glaring through the curtain. "You mean let them breed in their domination and trick fools into being grateful for it?"

"That system provided my pension!" Gramp's voice shifted. He was rising from the couch. "It's the only 'wealth' we got around here."

"*We* don't see a thin credit after you spend it pressing poison into your veins."

I'd heard all this crap a hundred times. I stood and stepped in front of Mom, in case Gramp wanted to take the argument nose-to-nose. Through the gap in the curtain, I saw his cheeks quivering while he considered the effort of escalating. "You get nothing, because those self-righteous 'unplanned' got no idea how to run a government."

"Instead of nurturing a healthy economy, our 'planned' leaders traded in corruption. We're suffering those consequences now."

Gramp craned his neck toward the kitchen unit, his face red.

"Old fool." Mom gritted her teeth.

I noticed Cam shoving deeper into his corner, his finger hovering over his drawing. He didn't remember when things were good, when we'd had our tidy little house, and Gramp was just a visitor bringing sweets and scary stories and irreverent jokes.

Mom followed the direction of my gaze. "I'm sorry." She rubbed her temples. "I don't know why I let him get to me."

"But you always do." I kissed her cheek to take the sting

from my words.

My thoughts shifted, sloshing through the fear of what I had to do. Nalen wasn't offering a solution. I wasn't stupid enough to believe that. But we needed a safety valve on this pressure, before it turned us into the worst versions of ourselves.

I STARED OVER THE PRECIPICE. A narrow path hugged the cliff face, disappearing beneath the shore break. Waves surged in and out of the Honeycomb, cavities and tunnels bored through the cliff base. The ground rumbled with warning, but I wasn't an idiot kid anymore, riding the ocean straights for a thrill. I was staying out of the water if I could help it.

The air held the brine of the sea—a cold, sharp hint of its vastness. I drew in a lungful and closed my eyes. I knew this place, my treacherous old playground. Its nooks, pools, and patterns were mapped in my blood.

The husk of Innovative Foods lay in the gloom behind me. I'd come here a lot when Mom worked there. The industry may have been shut down, but some of its creations had escaped the lab and sprouted in the natural world.

Stop stalling. Just do it.

I opened my eyes and stepped onto the path. Halfway down, I reached the mouth of the Honeycomb. Dank air misted from it like stale breath. I flipped up my wrist-vid and checked my timing. Then I shouldered my way inside, duckwalking until the opening narrowed to a tunnel. The light-seal I'd stuck to my forehead dimly illuminated my way. My pant knees grew soaked as I crawled through the passage. The waves didn't reach this high, but dampness puddled everywhere.

The echo of my breathing competed with the distant pound of waves, until a scuffling from behind drew me up short. I pricked my ears. Nothing. Probably just a burrow rat.

The passage angled down, growing increasingly steep. Twisting onto my butt, I slid to its base. The tunnel opened into an airy cave. A pool glistened at its center, eerily beautiful in the glow of my light. The water was glass-smooth. I soaked up its serenity but itched with the awareness that it wouldn't last.

The scuffling noise came again. I whirled around, this time sure it wasn't a rodent. I felt like my chest took a blow as a figure materialized in the cave's mouth.

"What's up, moondrop?"

I recognized the voice. My brain struggled to deny it as her shadow flowed into the cave. How the hells could a synth know about this? Oria might be soldier-bred but she was underaged—it was impossible that she was a cop. "What are you doing here?"

Her laugh rippled. "Following you, obviously."

"Not enough kicks for you on the southside?"

"Duller than dust." She was close enough for me to make out her face now.

"This isn't a playground. It's dangerous."

"Good. Not boring."

"Idiots drown down here all the time."

"I can take care of myself, moondrop."

"Why are you calling me that?" I asked, though I knew.

She pointed to the light-seal on my forehead. "You're glowing like one."

I narrowed my eyes. She gave me a closed-lipped smile.

A distant sound, like a pinging through pipes, chilled the sweat on my skin. Oria frowned and moved to the water's edge.

I twitched to move on, but if I went for the next stage, she'd follow. I couldn't expose my find.

The ping swelled to a cavernous groan, shaking loose my distraction. I'd never make the next tunnel's entrance now! Scouring the dark walls, I spotted a high cavity. I shot Oria a look. She stood, head cocked as though she were struggling to interpret the sound. *She has no idea what's about to hit her.*

I considered it, I admit. Easy solution to my problem.

She looked delicate against the pool's inky sheen, her white hair like muted moonglow. The water began to ripple.

"Oria."

She turned. I held out my hand. "Come on." She frowned. I wasn't grabbing her—she'd knock me flat—and I sure wasn't dying for her. I turned and leapt for the cavity's ledge, scrambling up. "Hurry!"

The groan built to a roar. I wedged my spine against the back of the cavity, just as the pool surged. My eyes hunted for Oria. She was airborne, then her hands caught the ledge. I grabbed her wrist, and she levered herself into the shelter.

"Hold tight!"

I gripped with my knees, my hands, every fiber of my body. Oria was rigid beside me. Icy water shocked over me, slamming me against the wall. Grit sanded my skin, my lungs burned and burned. Then the pressure dropped, as quickly as it had come. The water sank to my shoulders, and I gasped for air.

Oria's breathing steadied before mine. No doubt her cardio-vascular system was optimized. My lip curled.

"You considered leaving me down there, didn't you?"

Of course, I did. "Your gratitude is underwhelming. Not like I invited you to follow me." If that was really what she'd been doing.

"Thanks for the warning."

I couldn't tell if she was being sarcastic, so I didn't reply. Gods, it was cold. I gritted my teeth to keep them from chattering. My discomfort made me want to shut down, but I needed to think. There was no way Oria had followed me from Polly's Portables. She was here for a reason.

Snapping open my eyes, I twisted my head to look at her and found her eyes glinting, their silver glow fixed on me.

"Enhanced night vision," she said, her voice a shrug.

Unnerved, I looked away. "What are you really doing here? You didn't follow me."

"Untrue. I did follow you—after I saw you take the path down the cliff face."

"*Why?*"

"So much potential fun. Geysers, drop-offs, razor-toothed rodents, and *all kinds* of people up to naughty business."

My eyes widened—rage, not surprise. The synths were cutting in on the black-market euphoria fungus. They might be rich compared to us, but their fortunes had fallen. I glared into the dark. "You fucking synths take what you want. We can't stop you, but it feels good knowing they won't be manufacturing more of you."

"Does cussing make you feel powerful?" she asked, cool and bored.

Synths didn't seem to swear. Probably another form of snobbery, but I liked to imagine them short-circuiting if they tried. Not that they're androids, but I wasn't convinced there was much difference.

Oria laughed. "Such a revolutionary. You do know this tense little fiction we find ourselves living was written by someone else? You're just playing the role they wrote for you."

I knew exactly what she meant. Which pissed me off. "And you're just dying to hold my hand and sing the new unity anthem? You all think we're ugly subhumans." That she could see me clearly, while her face was only a blur to my eyes, pissed me off more.

"Naturally, every one of us was grown inside the same narrow-minded incubator."

I hated how childish I sounded, while she seemed so coolly mature—like her being smarter than me suddenly mattered in a deeper way. I let silence drop between us. There was no point in feeding her smug superiority.

"Your heartbeat is accelerated. Are you afraid of me?" Humor twined through her words.

"Sure," I steamed through my teeth.

"You think I'm a blood-drinking psycho, like everyone else."

I let a beat settle before I said, "So, is your father really one of The Fifty?"

"Yes." Clipped and cold. Her next words came in a gush. "Do you really imagine a crew of fifty soldiers had a synchronous, psychopathic breakdown?"

"Never thought about it." Satisfaction rushed through me; I'd finally cracked her cool.

"It would only take a handful to bring down that ship."

"Was your father one of that handful?"

"No one knows." Her voice was hollow. It made me shiver, but it also made me feel like an asshole.

"Not like you're his clone, right?"

"But I could be, no?" A feral smile curved her words. "Isn't that what disgusts you unplanned about us?"

"Whatever." My mistake for feeling a pinch of pity for her.

"Father wanted an ordinary daughter." A wisp of sadness

39

twined through her monotonal whisper. "But Moncreed tried to design me like him."

A failed experiment. That implication rippled goosebumps over my skin—a reaction to her sadness mixed in, but I didn't want to acknowledge it.

Silence resealed the cave while the water receded, millimeter by painful millimeter.

Finally, I judged it low enough and unwedged myself from the pocket. As I stiff-limbed my way out, Oria sprang down, landing with a squelch in the now ankle-deep water. I thumped after her, the water feeling almost warm as it re-soaked my shoes.

Now, how to shed Oria? She'd found my site. If I gave up now, it was lost for sure.

She crossed her arms. "Cut me in, moondrop."

I wasn't going to spar over the truth, not with so little time before the geyser reformed. "Why would I trust you?"

"I know you see us as a hive, but I *am* here alone."

Was she really? I strained my senses, hunting for another presence, but heard only the whistle of wind through the rock. "Go home."

"You know this place, but I'm the better climber."

That gave me pause. Her little demonstration at school. It hadn't been ego; she'd been proving her skill to me. Which meant she'd been planning this.

"You've followed me before."

She gave me her bladed smile. "It's perfect. We work together, split the take."

"What the hells do you need with the take? Your allowance not enough to get a new sharpener for your claws?"

"Suit yourself, but you'll have a hard time shaking me."

Her challenge angered me into stupidity. I stalked toward the next tunnel, clambering inside and crawling. Self-preservation demanded I check the geyser timing on my wrist-vid, but I wouldn't pause with every second counting. Oria was hot on my heels. At least if I drowned, I'd have the satisfaction of taking her with me.

Cool air tickled my face, and I detected the end of the tunnel by the deepening blackness. The rock began to vibrate. I pumped my hands and knees harder, until the skin felt rubbed raw. Finally, I reached the end, almost toppling onto my head at the abruptness. There was a drop of about a body length. My knees buckled as I landed, but I scrambled up and dashed for the wall. This cavern was funnel shaped, like a giant screw had bored it into the cliff.

I craned my neck as I climbed, hunting for the glow of my find. My breath hissed harshly, anxiety as much as exertion, but there it was—a faint, telltale shimmer far above. No one had snaked it. Yet. Oria was there, just below me. The geyser in this chamber was a seeper; pooling and climbing steadily beneath us.

My limbs ached, and I wasn't even halfway up. I'd never make it to the top. I'd been building my strength; it wouldn't be enough. Oria was level with me now, but I didn't look at her. I'd let her get to me at school. I couldn't now. I kept moving, biting my lip to ignore the acid burn of fatigue. The chamber narrowed and rock bit into my shoulder.

A ragged sigh snared my attention. Without meaning to, I glanced at Oria. She was watching me, teeth digging into her bottom lip. "I'll get it. You're too big to get a secure purchase up there."

My mouth thinned. The scrape on my shoulder stung as I reached for the next handhold.

"Bram." It was the first time she'd used my name. "We have to wait out the water, don't we?"

Yes, and it was insane to drain my strength in the climb. Up went my left arm as if disconnected from my brain.

"You're tough," she said, tense and urgent. "You're not stupid."

Up went my right.

"Idiot." Oria growled and surged upward like a cliff creature, so fast she seemed to fly.

I *was* an idiot. Tears stung my eyes, and still I climbed, falling further behind. As I inched my way up, I saw what her sharper eyes already had—the top was barely wide enough for her reedy frame.

I scanned around. What had I seen when I'd first scouted this site? Something closer to the bottom. Had another hunter snagged it, after all? Then I found it, like a smear of moonlight from behind thick clouds: another growth of pods. I frowned up at Oria, making sure she was occupied. The smaller find was only a body length above me, within reach. I strained my way up.

I squinted inside. The fungus had sprouted in a small pocket of rock, shriveled lumps knobbed over the stone. *Withered.* My stomach sank so hard I felt sick. Then I spotted a pitiful little glow. A single pod, its bottom puckered with decay, its bulb healthy. A stuttering exhale escaped between my frozen lips.

Digging my shoes deeper into their purchase, I gripped so hard with my right hand that it spasmed and reached with my left. The toothy opening to the pocket bit through my jacket.

Ignoring the pain, I shoved deeper. My fingers pincered the bulb and tugged. The pod was softer than I expected, and I nearly crushed it. Carefully, slowly, I withdrew it, fumble-fingering it into the inner pocket of my jacket with breath held.

My anchoring hand cramped, and panic stoppered my throat. The rock pressed in around me, the water below a black void waiting to swallow me.

"Bram," Oria's voice dropped thinly. "Don't fall."

I craned my neck, hunting for her gaze through the darkness.

My grip gave way, and I plunged down.

A second's chill rush, a jolting scrape against the wall, then frigid blackness stunned me. I was sucked down, too disoriented to try to swim. My feet struck bottom, and I finally had the sense to start kicking—through terrifying blackness, no certainty of up or down, lungs crying for air.

The water churned around me. Something touched me, and my mouth opened in a silent scream. Then a band wrapped around my waist, hauling me upward. Cold air slapped my face and I coughed desperately to receive it. As an infusion of air eased my panic, I registered the warm breath tickling my cheek.

"Stop struggling, before you drown us both." Oria's voice was gentle, her arms supporting me like a buoy. I couldn't speak as I met her eerily glinting eyes.

I CRAWLED over the cliff rise on boneless limbs. Oria had herded me up the path, keeping a hand on my battered jacket like she feared I'd topple over the side.

I shifted away from the ledge and planted myself in a slouch. My clothes were ice-slicked to my body, and everything hurt. Oria stood over me. Embarrassed, I couldn't meet her eyes.

When she moved on me, I was too stupid with fatigue to react. She crouched over me, shoving my chest, pushing me on my back against the cold ground. Her fingers nipped into my pocket and plucked out the pod. I gasped like a startled fish. Her fingers pushed against my mouth. Smooth, creamy sweetness burst over my tongue. It took me one horrified instant to process what she'd done. For a second, I thought of spitting the pod out. Too late. As its full impact hit, I knew I couldn't have spit it out for anything. Liquid pleasure melted me to the ground. I closed my eyes against it.

"I've watched you." Her warm breath misted my lips. "So *fucking* controlled. All the time. How does it feel to lose it?"

How had I trusted this creature? Even for a second? Rage swelled up my neck, making me feel like my head would burst with it. I snapped open my eyes, burning to shove her off, even knowing she could pummel me dead if she wanted. In that instant, I wanted her to. "This was a joke to you," I choked.

Her expression wasn't gloating. Nor angry. It was. . . weirdly fragile.

My fists unknotted, flopped to my sides. "You really are insane, aren't you?"

"I was riding high. Sheer adrenaline." Her eyelids dipped. "It was either that or kiss you."

Kiss me? An "ugly" thick-neck?

"Then you should have kissed me," I said through my teeth, relieved by a familiar, safer anger. "That pod could have fed my family for a month!"

Her expression didn't waver. "You don't have a monopoly

on suffering. I didn't choose to be born this way, less than you chose your own life."

"That makes no damned sense."

She studied me, the glitter of her silvery eyes giving me a twist in my chest. Then she shifted so close I could sense her body's warmth, just out of reach. My chill skin pebbled as if anticipating the contrast. "I see through you, moondrop. You *needed* that taste of indulgence."

A blush scalded my cheeks, startling me.

The stings and aches in my body had dulled, awash in my languid moondrop ease.

Rocking onto her heels, Oria said, "We're either competition. . . " She grabbed my hand. Before I could snatch it away, she reached into her jacket, pulled out three, fat, round pods—and rolled them onto my palm. ". . .or partners."

I felt as if she'd shoved me again, my mind stuttering to process what she'd offered.

"Your choice." Gaze growing diffuse, she added softly, "I was never your enemy."

Dizzied, I could only stare at her. I remembered the feel of her arm holding me in the water, the taut concern in her voice. *"Bram, don't fall."*

My fingers curved over the pods, slow and deliberate.

Oria's gaze fixed on my lips, then she uncoiled from me and dusted off her pants. I caught a sliver of a smile on her face as she turned toward the woods. "Later, moondrop."

I cupped the pods to my chest, probably worth enough to feed my family for months. It wasn't that possibility leaving me gaping at the star-streaked sky. *Partners.*

My lips tingled with the moondrop's aftereffect . . . or maybe something more.

Kara Stockinger is an alumnus of the Viable Paradise writing workshop and a member of the Writers' League of Texas. She spent part of her youth living in Japan and holds a doctorate in Japanese studies. Kara now resides in Austin, Texas, with her beloved husband and two children, working in the tech industry and escaping to science fiction and fantasy worlds whenever she can.

NOISE IN THE WOODS

By Britta Jensen

Noise had always bothered Lena. Yet nature's sounds had never felt like extraneous noise, until now. As she approached her grandfather's wood-and-cinderblock cabin tucked into the heavily forested woods, she felt like the trees were crashing into her. It probably didn't help that the pitch of the hill the cabin was built into made the pines and birches loom over Lena's thin frame. A buzzing started in the canopy as she passed by a group of ancient pines.

Normally the summer cicadas were a happy memory of her long afternoons spent with her grandfather, the vivacious bugs chirping merrily in the background. Now, at dusk, the sounds felt like the grinding of magical creatures about to seize her soul.

She lumbered up the stone steps of the cabin's porch. Birds flitted across in the pines above as she settled into a creaky rocking chair. There was a porch swing on the opposite side with a copse of birches leaning nearby, their leaves an electric green. The cicadas noised louder and she dug her phone out of her pocket to text her best friend, Nicolette: *When are you coming?*

She put her phone down, trying to imagine where Nicolette was in the three-story white-walled upscale salon where they'd worked for the past five years. She'd convinced her grandfather to get a haircut and hand massage there once.

"High-priced nonsense," her grandfather had said after his long white mane had been tamed into a shoulder-length cut during his free visit. Lena had hoped he'd be proud of her moving up in the world.

"I just want to see you more often, my dear."

Me too, Grandpa. I wish you were still here. A deep weight lodged in her chest.

He was all she had left of her family. Her parents both died in a motorcycle accident in southern Italy when she was fifteen. The cabin was what was left of her memories of any type of home.

She got up and plodded down the stairs, surveying the downtrodden cabin that really ought to have been modernized fifty years ago. The cicadas' chatter was drowning out any reasonable thoughts, a blooming pain now in her chest as she looked at the last of the gold-tinged sapphire sky fading behind the tall pines in the distance. She took out her keys and started toward the cabin's screen door, only to realize the locks were broken.

Grandpa probably kept forgetting his keys and thought this was better.

She opened both doors with a heavy sigh and creak of the hinges. On the kitchen table lay the documents the lawyer had sent over when she was still back in her apartment in Regensburg. She lifted up the bank statements under the documents, all in hers and Grandpa's names.

When did I open these? Had I?

She walked around the living room to see if anything else seemed out of place, cursing that she had not noticed the broken locks earlier. Each step reminded her she was going to need to replace the very creaky floorboards. After circling each room, nothing seemed to be missing. She sat on an ancient leather armchair she'd bought, her grandfather's only semi-comfortable piece of furniture. *I wish I'd brought more with me from my place.*

At first, two weeks ago, she had been loath to leave her tiny flat in Regensburg (that she could barely afford, Grandpa liked to remind her). But, when the lawyer confirmed she now owned her grandfather's property in her old village of Ursulapoppenricht, she felt a sudden switch inside. The narrow oppressiveness of Regensburg's tiny alleys, constant parade of tourists, and thick stone walls caused all traffic to reverberate, making the ancient city feel like an echo chamber instead of her home for the past fifteen years.

She wished, in that moment, looking up at the water stain on the golden wood ceiling, that she could talk over the renovations with grandfather, feel like she had permission to be here making all these decisions.

Her phone dinged with Nicolette's reply:

I'll be there tomorrow morning. We had a last-minute booking with that weird lady whose hair you permed last week. :(

Lena knew exactly who she was talking about. The soft-spoken women had come in for a full make-over on the anniversary of her daughter murdering her husband. After the woman shared full nude photos of both her boyfriends, Lena was desperate for a break from so many clamorous voices sharing intimate details she never asked for.

> What unnecessary details did she share with you this time?

> Looks like she's got a different boyfriend now!
> No pics, though xx

> Ohh, can't wait to hear tmrw!

Once it was dark out, Lena sat in the porch swing looking up at the stars. The cicadas had calmed down, and she heard a whistle sounding in the distance. The next closest neighbor was almost a kilometer away. A strange knocking started at the back door and she stopped, took a breath. *Just the wind.* The whistle that sounded again was just like her grandfather's. A rush of wind swept by, and the breeze carried a discharge of rain that shook the whole cabin.

"I don't know how I'm going to sleep tonight."

She walked back inside to the main washroom. A leak had already started over the bathtub. *Great, just when I thought I had a handle on the repairs.* She checked the rest of the cabin for any more leaks and luckily couldn't find anything else.

She sat on the orange wooden '70s couch her grandfather insisted helped with blood circulation in the back and put her head in her hands. The rolladens heaved and sighed in the sudden gusts of wind. *Please don't tell me everything is falling apart at once.*

Another knock came at the front door before a deluge

rained down. Lena opened the door to her elderly neighbors, Hans and Jutta. Her grandfather's oldest friends wore matching red parkas, their stooped figures dripping with rain. The white shock of their hair gave their ruddy faces an eerie glow.

"*Guten nacht, tut mir leid . . .* " Hans started apologizing for not calling.

"For some reason we don't have your number," Jutta continued.

They obviously forgot that only last week they'd called to tell me Grandpa died. "You called me last week," Lena said as neutrally as she could manage.

"Of course, of course." They looked strangely uncomfortable in the ancient awning.

"Please, come in from the rain. I'll start a fire." Lena gestured for them to come inside. She couldn't remember which side of the hill they were coming from. "I have some tea and biscuits here I brought from Regensburg."

They both looked shocked. "Regensburg, eh?" Hans said. "That's a long way off from these rural parts." He gave her a gap-toothed smile.

"It's less than an hour away, closer than Prague, for certain." She loved seeing local villagers' faces when she mentioned Prague, because so many had never been there, despite it only being a two-hour drive away. They preferred blaming their problems on the Czechs instead of seeing what they might learn from them.

"Might as well be another world compared to these beautiful woods," Jutta muttered.

I wonder why country people always assume their world is complete, as is? Lena thought. "Come take a seat. I'm sorry the chairs are not quite as comfortable as what I would have liked."

Jutta softened. "No, it's fine. I can see you already made changes in the last few days that make this place a lot better. Much homier than when Charles was here. God rest his soul." She crossed herself and bowed her head.

"I really miss him." Tears welled up in Lena's eyes and she brushed them away, not certain how her grandfather's old friends would feel.

Hans put his arm around Jutta. "Of course, of course. We came . . . to tell you . . . we want you to know you can rely upon us for anything you need. We are your closest neighbors, and we want to help you. We don't want you all alone here, day after day."

Lena nodded at them, glad for the offer, but unsure what they could help with, except choosing how to fix the leaks and renovate a place that had been standing for well over a hundred years.

"There's a leak in the bathroom over the tub . . . do you know of a roofer or someone who can fix that?"

"*Ja, ja.* I know of one. He's always so busy in the summer, though." Hans scratched his white chin stubble. "I might know of a patch that can hold over until he can take a good look."

Lena nodded, feeling suddenly very overwhelmed. *I have nowhere else to go.* She'd leased her flat in Regensburg to an eager American couple coming to the city for six months. She was now stuck, and she hated the feeling. Especially with the guilt she carried from not spending enough time with Grandpa in his last days.

"You look very tired, my dear. Can we bring you back to our place for some schnitzel, once the rain clears?" Jutta asked.

Lena thought on the idea. Could she stomach their

continual listing of all their ailments without her grandfather's banter to liven up the conversation?

She glanced around the dim light of the cabin and realized she had very little that was edible in the *kuhlshrank. A free meal is a free meal.* "Of course. Let me find my rain jacket." Through the large living room window, it looked like the rain was letting up across the vast, dark forest.

THE DESSERTS WERE LAID out on ancient plates decorated with pink roses, but Lena couldn't concentrate on the conversation. She kept hearing a soft singing combined with whistling above them. Yet, Jutta and Hans nattered on as though nothing was going on.

In an instant, the sounds stopped altogether, footsteps echoing on the granite stairs leading to the dining room. A very tall, somber man who looked to be in his thirties walked by without saying anything.

"*Gruss Gott*," Lena called out to him.

"Oh?" He turned back, noticing the strudel and marzipan treats. "Can I have some?"

"Of course, my dear," Jutta cooed, as though he were eight and not well above his thirties, on closer inspection.

His weathered face had crow's feet at the edges of his eyes. He avoided all eye contact with everyone, intent on the sweets, smacking them as he ate, revealing yellowed and slightly rotten teeth.

"This is our nephew, Marko. He repairs motorcycles. He's quite the genius," Jutta said.

Hans hmphed in response to this.

"Nice to meet you, Marko." Lena held out her hand.

Marko ignored it.

After he'd finished, he wiped his hands on his trousers and left without another word, flipping his long brown hair over his shoulder.

Jutta leaned into Lena, whispering. "We were hoping you could cut that hair of his, make him look a bit more respectable?"

When Lena considered this, Jutta spoke a little louder. "You still work at that fancy salon, don't you?"

When Marko re-entered and stomped up the stairs with an antisocial air that froze the room, Lena was glad to refuse. "Oh, I'm off work the next six months. But, I'm happy to recommend a colleague at the salon."

They would never venture to Regensburg for a haircut, she was certain.

Jutta pouted, crossing her arms. "Oh, can't you just do it here in the kitchen?"

Lena saw she was used to often getting her own way, especially from the tight lips on Hans' glowering face.

"No, it isn't possible." She let the directness of it sit there as Jutta bristled and exhaled. Hans patted her shoulder before retreating to the kitchen.

Lena passed a piece of strudel to Jutta. "I love this sitting room. How did you decide on the decorations?"

Jutta was off, nattering on, while Lena nodded, a tug of grief pulling her down into the shadowlands as she gazed into the darkness beyond the net curtains.

THE NEXT MORNING, Lena was overjoyed to see Nicolette's lovely froth of curls bounding up the wooded path leading to the top of Mariahilfberg.

"Lena!" Nicolette cried out. Lena was engulfed in Nicolette's halo of tawny curls as her best friend embraced her, not letting her go when Lena tried to step away.

"How are you, my dear Lena? It feels like ages since I've seen you."

"It's only been days, Nic . . ." Lena had to smile. Nicolette's way of exaggerating inconsequential things was part of her charm.

Nicolette held Lena at arm's length, her large brown eyes taking in Lena's slight, tall frame and bleached blonde hair. Lena was sure she was looking for all the things Lena couldn't hide from her. "Let's get lost in the woods, and then you'll tell me, won't you?" Nicolette pushed them onward and Lena was glad for her commanding presence. They had bonded in *Real Schule* with a deep understanding about what it was like to be both foreign and German.

Lena filled her in on the delightful, but quirky Ursulapoppenricht neighborhood on the hillside, and the weirdness of Jutta and Hans' nephew.

"No way . . . *echt?*

"*Stimmt* . . . yeah, he's the nephew of my Grandpa's neighbors."

"Now *your* neighbors."

"So, it would seem," Lena said. They stopped in the middle of the cool, green woods, modern life completely behind them. Lena looked up at the fast-moving clouds above, allowing brief glimpses of cornflower blue sky. The only sounds were the bird call and woodpeckers above them, and a slight crunching sound in the distance. Lena kept moving past the lime green ferns brushing at her sweater. The further they moved, the more the pines and stark white birches seemed to insulate them from the outside world.

"I think we're the only ones here," Lena said, stopping to catch her breath by a fallen tree trunk, its branches spread across the ferns and saplings rising out of its corpse in the faint daylight. A bird called above them. She couldn't help thinking about that whistling sound, how it had kept her from sleeping the previous night. She had tossed and turned, imagining someone trying to break in, and because the sound was unidentifiable, it only bothered her more.

She tried filling Nicolette in as they continued on the trail. "I wish I knew who was trying to scare me. And why."

Nicolette's eyes widened, and she stepped closer to Lena. A tall man with two long, brown braids in full Bayern *trachtenwear* stomped toward them. His lederhosen top crisscrossed his wide chest, but Lena was puzzled by their attachment to what looked like a leather kilt. *How uncomfortable.* She kept staring, trying to make sure she wasn't mistaken as she scanned his traditional checked blue shirt and leather lederhosen top that had been adjusted to fit the leather skirt pleated to the tops of his knees.

She would have laughed in another circumstance, but the look on his shadowed face was so grim she felt the urge to bolt.

"Should we continue, or let him pass?" Nicolette asked. Lena felt a tension in her voice she hadn't heard before. *She's spooked, too.*

"Let's stay here, let him pass." Lena stepped further into the ferns around them, closer to the mint green branches of the sapling. She picked up a large branch, hoping he would continue tromping in his knee-high boots that were only getting louder. *If not, I've got this for defense.*

"*Gruss Gott,*" he called out.

"Hallo. . ." Lena weakly replied. *Please let him just continue onward.* But, as he got closer, she caught a sense of familiarity in him. It was Jutta's nephew, Marko.

Great, I have to try to make some sort of polite conversation with the sullen dude.

She turned away, but Nicolette was onto her. "What is it?"

"Later."

Marko stopped in front of them. "You're Lena, right?"

"Why are you asking?" Nicolette stood straighter, even though the man was a good two heads taller than her. "Nice skirt, by the way."

Marko looked down at his kilt, puzzled. "Genuine Bavarian tribal wear. It's what real men of this area are supposed to wear, didn't you know?" He folded his arms, looking too much like Lena's old high school teacher.

"Right." Nicolette said thinly.

"You two are clearly half *Auslanders*, so you don't understand." Marko said with no malice, directing his dark gaze at both of them.

"You're not supposed to say things like that anymore," Lena said. "It's rude."

"It's true, isn't it?" He pointed at Lena. "You're only half German." He then gestured toward Nicolette. "I have no idea what she is."

Lena's blood boiled. "Stop. You can't talk to us like this. *Auslander* is an offensive word. You're old enough to know that." She let that sink in. "There are no true Germans. We're all mixed."

Marko coughed and crossed his arms, looking cold as the sunlight was blocked out by thick clouds overhead. He glanced around the forest, seeming to want to say more.

Nicolette leaned in to Marko. "Maybe you should spend more time actually reading books instead of playing video games."

Lena coughed to keep herself from laughing. When they were younger, they'd encountered this sort of jeering from native-born Germans all the time, especially those with little exposure to the outside world.

Marko took one step toward them.

Lena raised the branch between them.

"It isn't safe for you in the cabin. Find another place to stay. Too many ghosts there." He waved his hand as though he were warding something off.

A mist descended gently from the pines above them. He trudged off quickly, the mist curling behind him and quickly making him seem to disappear.

Lena stared at the whole scene, wondering if she had just imagined it. The bark from the branch made her palms itch and confirmed that she was truly awake.

"You cannot make this shit up. What was that?" Nicolette asked.

"He doesn't realize his threats mean nothing to me," Lena said, letting the branch fall before finding one with less bark. "He doesn't frighten me."

"Was he like this yesterday?"

Lena couldn't help laughing. "Worse. He barely said anything, while still managing to change the mood of the entire room. Totally creepy." She grasped the smoother new branch in her palm. "I'm never going back to his aunt and uncle's house."

"Of course not. In fact, we're going to continue our hike, then I'm staying with you tonight," Nicolette insisted, leading them opposite where Marko had tromped off. "After his bizarro warning, we're definitely replacing those locks in the cabin, pronto!"

The mist folded behind as the hush of the forest curled around them. Lena was truly afraid Marko was going to reappear at any point, possibly floating above them as some type of phantom. For the first time, it was uncomfortable to be amongst the quiet of nature. A strange fluttering starting in her stomach, gnawing at her the whole way up the hill.

She and Nicolette emerged a half hour later at the top of Mariahilfberg again, the yellow stones of the ancient church in stark contrast to the grey sky. Lena was thankful to see civilization again. *Who would have thought such a change could come over me?* She looked behind them, back into the deep, green forest where the mist obscured their trail. She watched for a few minutes, making certain they hadn't been followed.

Nicolette suggested they try to see if one of the handymen she knew might have a lock for sale, since it was Sunday and everything except cafes and restaurants were closed.

After several hours of trying, they gave up and picked up some takeout doner kebab that Nicolette was always the best at picking. It helped she was half-Algerian and could still speak a fair bit of Arabic and French. The shop guys often threw in extra tzatziki or rice in hopes of getting Nic's number.

Lena couldn't wait to dive in and catch up with Nicolette in the cabin, but when they arrived, Hans was smoking a pipe on the porch, gliding away in the rocking chair as though he didn't have a care in the world.

Jutta bustled out of the front door and settled herself primly onto the porch swing. A faint whistling started in the woods behind them, but neither seemed to notice.

Strange, Lena thought.

Nicolette narrowed her eyes at them. "Do they think they own the place now that their best friend is gone? Or, do they think you're some *Auslander* pushover?" Lena could see she was gearing up for the same fight Lena anticipated was brewing. Lena gingerly walked up the gravel walkway.

"Jutta, Hans. . . is there a reason you're making yourselves so welcome on my porch?"

"Oh . . . well . . ." Jutta started to fidget, wringing her hands as she swung on the porch swing. "Your grandfather—"

Hans cut her off. "He said we could come anytime we wanted. It's why the locks don't work. He wanted it to be a community property, you see." Hans stood up, folding his arms.

"That's not stated anywhere in his will." Lena carefully made her way up the steps, her stomach already turning from the conflict. "And even if it had been stated in his will, the property belongs to me. I can't just waltz over to your house and sit in your sitting room any day I please."

"You're always welcome," Jutta brightened, laying back on the swing, looking less like an octogenarian with her short cropped white hair, and more like a schoolgirl having a lark.

"I need you both to leave." Lena insisted. Nicolette stood very close to her, putting her arm around Lena. "Now."

Hans shuffled upward, followed by Jutta. They took their time making their way down the steps, looking like they were milking the moment.

"And tell your nephew to stop trying to intimidate me."

At that, the two of them stiffened and turned around to face Lena, giving her scrunched looks of incomprehension before continuing quickly down the hill.

"Let's eat here on the porch. I want to feel like we can take advantage of the nice weather, while it lasts," Lena said.

"And watch out for bored busybodies." Nicolette bounced her dark eyebrows at Lena before they tucked into the spread of delicious spiced meats, rice, tzatziki, and fries. It was the sort of meal her grandfather would have appreciated.

She lifted a glass of *apfelschorle* to Nicolette's beer. "In Grandpa's memory!"

"*Prost!*"

LENA HAD SETTLED into sleep next to Nicolette in her grandfather's old room. The strange whistling had started up, and departed from the tunes her grandfather usually whistled, after they finished dinner. She had been too tired to try and identify where it was coming from. She and Nicolette had shoved the living room furniture against both the front and back doors before heading off to sleep.

Lena drifted in a dream of mist. She was back in the forest, her grandfather whistling his favorite futbol anthem from Bayern Munchen. She felt the earth beneath her dropping, crumbling away into a fast-moving mist that sucked at her feet as the whistling got louder.

LENA WOKE to the sound of whistling, except in a completely different tune from her dream.

Nicolette shot up, jostling Lena. "Are you whistling?"

"No." Lena rubbed her eyes. "Of course not."

Nicolette slipped on her socks, tugging at the ancient wooden rolladens so that a sliver of light peeked through each window. The clock on the wall indicated it was three in the morning.

Lena's grandfather always said that was the witching hour. *Well, let's go get some witches, then.*

She crossed the room to the cabinet where her grandfather's hunting rifle lay. The whistling continued even closer and more haunting. She grabbed the rifle.

"What do you want me to do?" Nicolette asked, rustling through the belongings on the ground and finding an old lantern. She quickly lit it while Lena made sure the mechanism on the gun was still working. It didn't have any bullets, but whoever was out on the porch didn't know that.

The whistling turned shrill as they approached the front door. "We're going to have to be quick in order to see who it is."

"What if it's some creature?" Nicolette asked.

Oh, that imagination of hers.

"Right. We'll scare that too." Lena pointed to the rocking chair blocking the front door. It had moved several inches from where they'd placed it earlier, the door slowly opening as the whistling died away.

Sweat rolled down Lena's back, despite the cool night air seeping into the cabin. The front porch light flicked and went out as a figure attempted to make its way through the front door.

"Stop!" Lena called out, smacking them in the chest with the butt of the gun.

She heard a groan as Nicolette rushed at them with her lamp. "Who are you? Who do you think you are that you can just burst in here?"

The man was dressed entirely in black, his hoodie obscuring his face. Lena swatted at him again as he burst back through the door. *He's got the same build as Marko*, she thought.

"Marko, I know it's you!!!" Lena screamed as the sound of a motorcycle started up. She ran after him as he made his getaway.

"We didn't get his license plate number." Nicolette followed down the narrow gravel path with her mobile.

"He probably doesn't have one."

"Maybe crossed the border from Czech?" Nicolette offered.

"We both know it's Marko." They both started laughing.

"You really know how to swing that thing, don't you?" Nicolette said, approaching the gun carefully. At the salon, Nicolette was known for being the boldest with difficult customers. Lena liked seeing a reversal here, though she didn't relish having to replace those locks herself in the morning.

She dialed the police to report what had happened, with Nicolette filling in any missing details. It was the weekend; the police probably wouldn't show until the next day.

"Should we just sit on the porch with that thing and scare the locals for a while?" Nicolette offered, a gleam in her eye.

"Yeah, it's almost four in the morning, we've got nothing better to do until the stores open." Lena grabbed the gun and a few quilts, closing the door behind her before settling on the porch swing. Nicolette joined her with two tumblers and some gin and tonic.

"Why not?" Lena said, clinking the glasses. "To Grandpa, may he rest in peace and protect us from harm."

"Amen." Nicolette downed her portion in one loud slug.

LENA STOOD WITH NICOLETTE, both of them still in their flannel pajamas, reviewing the options the OBI store helper was offering them at the lock counter. Unlike Lena's experiences in America and Nicolette's in France, he was very good at pointing out what was on sale and the honest quality of the fifteen odd locks that would fit her grandfather's door.

"A break-in, you say?" He asked, looking very curious.

"Yeah, when I arrived to take over his cabin. The neighbors said he never locked his doors anyway."

"Really?" The guy seemed baffled. "Ursulapoppenricht, you say?"

"Yeah, but it's deeper into the woods, outside the main town."

"Then you definitely need locks; ignore the neighbors. Seems shady to me." He identified two brands and placed them both in their hands. "Take a look, let me know if you have more questions." He breezed away, helping a foreigner who clearly spoke zero German.

Lena found it amusing how many of her half countrymen had homesteaded in Germany, sometimes upwards of twenty years, but still spoke barely passible German to do everyday tasks. *My Papa had certainly been like that.*

HALFWAY THROUGH THE LOCK INSTALLATION, with the help of Mikael, the OBI employee who'd helped them that morning, Jutta came bursting up the hill, her hands full of a roll of papers.

"Lena!" She bellowed. "What exactly are you doing?"

Lena told Mikael to continue while Nicolette watched on with curiosity and a slight smile at the edge of her mouth. "Installing the locks, of course. There was a break-in last night." Lena brought her palms together. "But it sounds like you already know that, since the assailant looked an awful lot like Marko."

Jutta stopped, shock coloring her pale face bright red. Nicolette stepped off the porch while Jutta stared at her, baffled by Nicolette's dark appearance, it was obvious.

"This is my best friend and colleague, Nicolette. You briefly met yesterday." Lena offered, smiling, because it looked like Jutta was up to something by the fistful of papers in her hands.

"*Ja, ja*. Nice to meet you." She waved Nicolette's offered hand away. "I have here your grandfather's remaining documents he left in my trust. It clearly says that the cabin cannot have locks, that he meant it to be a community property so we could all enjoy it. See, right here . . ."

Lena swiped the papers out of Jutta's grasp. "I'll take them to the lawyer, no problem, Jutta. Meanwhile, this is *my* property. Not yours, not the community's. I'm happy to socialize and share the garden and blackberries you all enjoy, but if I want my door locked so a strange man doesn't break in, I have the right. Don't you think?"

Jutta stood there, mouth open, shuffling from one foot to the other. "Don't you trust us? We were your grandfather's best friends. He was like a brother to us. You grew up with all of us around you. Have you forgotten where you come from?"

Lena sighed. People in the village only mentioned her forgetting where she came from when it was convenient for them. Otherwise, she was ever and always the *Auslander*. She turned her attention back to Mikael, who was finishing the last touches on the lock.

"All done," he said. Lena strode over to pay him the two hundred euros for installation on both doors. He happily curled the notes into his pocket and waved gregariously at them as he made his way back to his car. That was one advantage of her being half-American: she knew how to overpay for things she had no desire to do.

Jutta was still fuming on the steps, and Lena was so tired and overwrought that she handed the papers to Nicolette.

"Jutta, go home." Lena stood there, staring at the old woman's milky green eyes. All the happy memories with her faded into a soupy mass that lodged in her chest.

"Maybe you should have rethought encouraging your nephew to act like an idiot," Nicolette said.

Jutta turned on her heels when she saw she was outnumbered. Lena watched her stooped figure retreat across the lawn and into her three-story house that could have fit two of Lena's cabins into it.

"That woman is a piece of work," Nicolette said, folding her arms, not minding she was crumpling the papers Lena suspected had been doctored.

"She might be, but I'll let the lawyer deal with her. We have better things to think about." Lena handed Nicolette the spare key and the two of them happily locked the doors behind them.

They fired up Lena's old laptop and schemed about their upcoming trip to Spain. If the cabin needed so many renovations to make it livable, and Lena couldn't return to her flat, she might as well enjoy some time on the Mediterranean trying to resolve the grief weighing on her.

"Let's stay as far away from spooky people as possible," Lena said. Nicolette put her arms around her, letting her tears fall without saying a word.

Two WEEKS LATER, the renovators were coming, the fence already built, and Lena took one last look at her boxy luggage. It was an old relic from her grandfather, but still serviceable.

"You sure that's going to hold everything?" Nicolette asked from where she glided on the swing seat on the porch.

"Oh, yeah. It'll be fine. I don't need much on the shores of Barcelona!" Lena smiled, and it felt genuine and good. She needed to sit with the memories of her grandfather for a bit and there was no better place than the ocean and sights of Barcelona to help sort her cares.

Daylight was coming up over the horizon as they waited for Nicolette's brother to take them to the Nürnberg airport. A faint whistling started in the woods behind them.

"Probably a jackal. They're coming back you know?" Nicolette said. "I saw one driving here. Thought it was a fox."

"I don't know, it could be Marko, being an idiot again." Lena grumbled.

They looked at each other and after a few seconds, simultaneously yelled "Marko! Stop!" The whistling ceased immediately.

Lena's phone dinged, and she took it out of her pocket. The lawyer had just written with the final deed on the cabin. Jutta and Hans' names weren't mentioned at all. *Not intended as a community property after all.*

"Let the jackals keep making their crazy sounds. It won't stop us from enjoying ourselves, eh?" Lena took her best friend in her arms, holding her close and letting Nicolette read off the screen. When she finished, she let out a victorious whoop that caused a few lights to come on in the sleepy village below.

BRITTA JENSEN'S NOVEL, *Eloia Born,* won the 2019 Writers League of Texas YA Discovery Prize. Her stories explore themes of persevering through disability, found family, and the intersection of various cultures on real and imagined worlds. Other published works include *Hirana's War, Ghosts of Yokosuka,* and her short story, "Why Not Ophelia?" in the *Castle of Horror Anthology Volume 6: Femme Fatales.* For the past twenty years, Britta has edited books and taught creative writing. She lived in Japan, South Korea, and Germany for twenty-two years before settling in Austin, Texas, with her awesome husband. You can learn more about her work at www.brittajensen.com.

STATIC ROAD

By Ishita Fernandes

We are the only car on this unlit single-track road. Two yellow beams reflect an endless sea of swirling insects suspended and inhabiting every inch of air, colliding at random, in a moonless Mombasa night. Everything that is alive in the humid darkness had found its way to our solitary headlights, like a thickly moving veil. Damp hot air fills my lungs and salty sweat beads sting the skin around my nose. Palm leaves scrape the doors. A crack sounds from the suspension as we bounce over a rock, landing with a shuddering thud.

"We should have waited until a full moon," Jerry says, itching his stubble and giving out a long yawn.

"Thanks, Jerry, that is enormously helpful," I reply, scratching a new bite at the back of my sticky neck.

I have been driving for almost nine hours, exhausted and irritable, hoping we would find the house soon. I am starting to think this might be an expensive waste of time. These trips are never easy, but after this I will have the payoff I desperately need, and life might become more bearable. It's not just about getting there first. I am tired of being branded as a "lost cause" for as long as I can remember. It's about time I turned my luck.

Nothing has prepared me for the unpopulated road which hisses with life like TV static. Thankfully, we rolled up our windows further up the road—hopefully too many mosquitos haven't seeped in. Jerry seems to be almost immune to them.

"Apparently, bugs don't like it when you have a lot of vitamin B. I opted to include Marmite in my survival pack. Great for stamina too." He says this with a wink.

A pinprick on my leg and another on my neck."I wish I could love Marmite," I reply.

The shock absorbers are worn. We have felt each bump since leaving Thika. I have stayed in third gear for the most part.

Our 1985 Nissan Cherry reeks of melting plastic and body sweat. Earlier, I tried the knob on the AC that expelled a loud rattle and a pungent sulphuric odour. The dirty seats vibrate, and the tattered material makes me want to scratch my bare legs. They were described as velour in the ad; these old models must have been comfortable at some point. The seats sag in the centre while a spring digs into my spine.

I crunch down to second gear as the sea of dancing insects makes visibility almost impossible. My T-shirt sticks to my back and pits. My left bra strap irritates me, slipping every so often. I ask Jerry to unclasp it from the back, which he is more than willing to do. I release the straps from my shoulders, keeping one hand on the wheel. Pulling my bra through the T-shirt sleeve opening, I free myself of its constraints, propelling it out of the window and into the swirl. I imagine a tiger leaping up to grab it in his teeth. As I glance in the rearview, it has been flung into the darkness of the bush.

"We should be there soon, Soph. Just keep driving slow . . ." murmurs Jerry, his neck nodding forward in half-sleep.

I turn to him. "How far is it?"

"Close . . . five minutes, I think. We should be there in good time," he says, struggling to keep awake.

No satnav. His guess is as good as mine.

"You wanted authentic right? You won't get much more than this," he says, almost reading my mind before his eyes draw shut.

Minutes have passed. We must be close. I almost dread this moment. I am not someone who likes betrayal, but the six-figure prize money will be life-changing. It's not easy when it's been the two of us for so long. Comrades in arms, as he calls it. There will be consequences with his temper, which can ignite without an excuse. I have to get this right, and I need to be quick.

I purposely turn off the ignition key. The car protests, rattling violently, and then stalls in gear, waking Jerry. The loot from the last job jangles in the boot.

"Jerry, man, I can't believe it. Go check—see what the hell it is!" I shout. "Something just on the side must have jammed into the tyre." I curse repeatedly, until he gets out.

The door creaks open against the thick foliage, with just enough of a gap for a lanky guy like Jerry to squeeze out. He moves to the front so I can see him in my headlights and holds his hand up. His limp blond hair sticks to his moist face, his eyes are deep-set and bloodshot. I can't look much better; it's been a full nine hours since we both last ate, and that was a small local maize dish and a Coke at the last truck stop. After one whiff of the facilities, I relieved myself in the bush.

"I can't see anything, Soph. I bloody told you to go slow."
He peers down the side of the car.

"Check the front bumper!" My pulse quickens, every beat
pressing heavily inside my chest. He raises his hands to say OK
and bends to inspect the damage. A large part of me knows I'll
regret this, but for now this is what I need to do—stay focused
on the outcome. It may be the only chance I have. I can hear
him fiddling with the front bumper.

"I can't really see what the issue is, Soph," he says, still
crouched down and out of view.

"Keep looking." Can he detect the tremor in my voice? I
don't have a second to lose.

I seize the moment. Turning the key, I press the accelerator
so hard I fear my foot will tear through the floor. The front
lights crack, the wheels spin in the dirt as he falls backward,
groaning. My wheels bump over him as I drive forward. The car
lurches upward, the full force jolting my head and knocking it
sharply against the steering. A loud thwack below me, like the
sound of wood splintering. Every fibre inside me wants to take
my foot off the accelerator.

Keep going, don't stop. A voice inside me urges me forward,
muting my instinct to hit the brakes. My hands quiver on the
steering as I struggle to keep to a straight path. I wipe my forehead. Am I bleeding? My eyes dart across the road ahead,
looking for anyone who could have witnessed my betrayal.
Driving without lights, I crunch into first gear, then downhill
into neutral, letting the car rattle downward on its own momen-
tum. Checking the rearview and then my beaten side mirrors for
signs of movement, I see nothing but a dark void, and yet I feel
watched. There is a lit building ahead, and I use it to navigate
through the darkness. The house is occupied, and I am ready.

I push into gear, accelerating harder until the car shudders. My head is pulsating, counting down the moments. I slow down fast enough not to hit the front porch. I climb the heavy steps of this old concrete-built house, nearly tripping over an old chair strewn the floor covered in dried palm leaves. The buzz around me intensifies.

I reach for the door handle and open it to find a bright and welcoming light shimmering into my eyes. I must have made it with only seconds to spare. Illuminated letters hang in midair, surrounded by a yellow halo, forming the words 'LEVEL 33.'

No one has ever made it this far! The words spin around to make their point, bouncing ever so slightly. A wave of relief hits me as I take large deep breaths, steadying my balance. I wait for it, and it never disappoints. The room echoes with the sound of a coin drop just like winning big at the slots. That will be the loot, filling up my bank account as we speak. Double the money now that Jerry hasn't made the cut.

As the light dims, the words are replaced by three options suspended in front of me: PLAY, PAUSE, or STOP. I touch PAUSE and take off my visor and mouthpiece; the air changes as my eyes meet the pale blue peeling wallpaper.

I am back in the familiar sounds and smells of my South London flat. I squint as my eyes tear, adjusting to the afternoon light and the sounds of the housing estate—a police siren and a mother calling her child in the dwelling below. My brain takes a moment to catch up, and I can still see an outline of the open door, which disappears after a second.

I unclench my fists from the gaming steering wheel and unstrap my feet from the stirrups of my Rifter that has stopped moving my feet on the spot. Time to take a break.

My tongue feels like sandpaper. I pull off my rubber shoes

and my moist bare feet touch the cold lino. I almost trip over walking across the gritty floor to the lounge, passing the stained mushroom-coloured sofa to the kitchen. I feel the urge to scratch at the simulated bite at the back of my head. I know this odd feeling will leave me soon enough, but right now I feel like an uncoordinated mess.

Using my fingers, I comb through my knotted red hair. Long stray strands surrender themselves without any force, falling to the floor. Behind me, I can hear the familiar clicking of the Rifter calling me back in.

I unzip my sensory suit, throwing the colostomy bag and urine sack with my body waste into the kitchen bin, my hands still trembling. Pulling open the kitchen drawer, I find the replacement bags. Wiping myself down with a kitchen roll, I rezip myself into my suit again. I have it down now to less than fifty seconds. No time for toilet breaks.

The kitchen tap drips rhythmically. The ketchup-stained dishes are piled up in an unruly, Jenga-like stack. I open the fridge, which gives out a moan, to find a limp piece of ham. It's the last watery piece in the plastic pack. I force it into my mouth unceremoniously. Salty and slippery, it feels less than satisfying.

I repeat my daily mantra in my head: *Winning will make the difference.* Only one more day of this. Staying in pole position will require focus. I want to reimagine what I could do with that kind of cash. My needs are basic. I only hope it will mean not living here, on this estate, ten floors up with a broken lift. I could get shot of Mum and her latest ogre, Davy. Lately, he'd been using the bottom half of his palm to give him maximum impact without bruising.

Leon at the cafe could have worked it out. I flinch sometimes on busy nights when I need to bend to clean the grill. The part of me that hoped he would notice, step in, maybe ask me if everything is OK at home, gave up months ago. He either isn't nosey enough or doesn't want to bother getting involved. He asked me for a one-to-one after the staff huddle one morning. I thought he might bring up the gash on my hand, only to tell me a customer had complained about my personal hygiene, recommending a cheap roll-on.

Most days, I walk around the café like someone in a trance. If it wasn't for the money, the Rifter and its accessories would have been sold already, by Mum or Davey. They have threatened it a thousand times, but Jerry has paid them off to have it sitting in our living room.

If I win, no—*when* I win—I will take little Chloe with me, and that is a certainty. I could give her what I never had, starting with that play castle she's been longing for and maybe that other thing. What was I thinking about?

The thought is lost; I shake my head to refocus. The counter begins again in the room, emanating from the Rifter that pulsates urgently. I hold my hair back in a bunch with one hand, open the tap, and with my mouth under it, take in large gulps, the runoff water trickles down my rubber suit. I straighten too quickly, and the room feels like it's tilting. The acrid taste of bile and ham threatens its way up my throat before I suppress it again.

Pacing back to the Rifter, I pull the rubber shoes back on and strap my feet into the stirrups. My hands tighten on the steering wheel. As I reach for my visor, there is a familiar slow double-knock at the door, and then the inevitable.

"I know you are in there, Soph. Fuck, Soph, why? I only got you that damn Rifter, and the bloody suit, so you could help me win. Help *us* win. What happened to *together,* Soph? What happened to *fifty-fifty*?"

A pause.

"Was that *all bullshit*? You ungrateful bitch. I know you are in there. I owe money for that Rifter!" He raps harder on the door. "Either you pay, or your little sis will. *Sophie!*"

"Sorry, Jerry. Please understand." I say it even though I know pleading won't work; we had a deal. Another heavy thump and the door to the flat shudders. The locks might hold. I saw the police enter the flat a few doors down, and they needed one of those large metal battering rams. I just hope that mine is strong enough to withstand Jerry. The countdown has already started, but I can hear him kicking stronger and harder now. I insert my mouthpiece and place the visor over my face. My skin feels immediately warmer.

I am back in the game and the dimly lit house; the air has changed; it is thick with humidity and a heavy sweet sickly scent of the African bush. Jerry's loud thumping is barely audible and feels like it is somewhere far off in the distance, concealed by the swirling hiss of the bush beyond.

I look for the three options that were previously hanging in front of me, PLAY, PAUSE, and STOP, but I see nothing. Has the game already started? I can't tell. The banging in the distance has stopped. It feels like instinct, but something is off.

I pull off my visor and I am back in the flat, spitting out the mouthpiece. Jerry is standing in front of me, his hair stuck to his face, eyes darkened. This is the Jerry I know, and I can read that look. It's not just anger, it's betrayal.

He looks the worse for wear. His eyes are deep-set and sunken, his skin stretched thinly across his face, so you can see the angles of his cheekbones. The game has taken its toll.

"Sorry, Jerry, but you must understand. You of *all* people know how desperate I am." I hold out my arm. My feet are still strapped into the Rifter, but he reads me.

"I won't hurt you while you are on that. I don't want to damage it. Got to return it, see! I still owe money for it." His voice is shaking. Wet cheeks and bloodshot eyes.

"No one needs to get hurt," I say softly, but I already know how this will play out.

"Really? Well, I beg to differ. See, we are partners, right. I picked you for this based on your skill. *You* needed money. I am the one who sent your mum and her boyfriend away on the trip to Bournemouth this week with your baby sis, so *you* could focus on this. That is what partners do. I was generous enough to give you a fifty-fifty split, you stupid cow." His hand is in a fist and, as I notice it, he pulls it behind his back.

"Soph, get off the Rifter." I comply and undo the foot straps carefully, all the while keeping my eyes on Jerry.

"I can finish the game, Jerry. Think about it. I will split what I win."

"Enough with the lies, Soph. You would do anything now. I know that. I can't trust a thing that comes out of your mouth!" *He has a point.*

I can hear the lady downstairs singing to her baby, but I don't recognise the tune or the language. The soiled net curtain from the open window lifts and balloons outward into the room with a sudden breeze, kissing Jerry's arm and catching him by surprise. As he turns toward it, I jump off the Rifter toward the kitchen.

I am only a few feet into the kitchen, and he pulls me back by my hair, pushing me hard against the sink. His hands are already around my neck; I can't breathe. My gasps for air are futile. I want to beg him to stop but nothing comes out.

I push at his hands, but he is remarkably strong. I scratch at his fingers in the hope of some release, but he grips tighter. Jerry's face is so close to mine, I can see the beads of sweat on his brow, the sickly sour scent of his breath, the determination in his eyes.

Jerry is moaning—no, crying—as my gasps slow. The overflowing sink of dishes behind me rattles. As he twists his hands harder, the skin on my neck burns in agony. The room dims. I let my arms drop to my sides into the sink. My outstretched fingers meet the coolness of the gritty dishwater. Will this be my last thought, the last feeling of my life in this grim world?

I can feel a cold metal object in the water. Wrapping my fingers around it, I use the last of my strength to raise my trembling hand up from the basin, lashing it through the air with as much force as I can gather.

The shock in Jerry's eyes is immediate. He lets out a visceral wail. Stumbling back, he screams again, the blood pouring freely from his neck like an open tap, spilling its contents across the kitchen floor. His fingers clutch on his neck, barely able to contain it. He is desperately trying to remove the knife which is lodged deep into his neck.

My legs weaken, and I slide down against the cabinet, still gasping for air.

I watch him as he moves erratically. Knocking the kitchen bin, his feet slide on its contents and the colostomy bag. He continues his screams. I can sense his agony and the nausea rises inside me again. I see it in slow motion as he loses his footing, knocking his head onto the radiator with a hard crack. A quick succession of sharp breaths followed by slow shallow ones as his chest rises and falls, then stillness. His skin and hair are streaked in crimson.

I try to remain conscious, taking deeper breaths. Behind me, the tap continues its relentless drumming. My neck burns, as though Jerry's fingers are still wrapped around it, but he is slumped on the floor in front of me, unmoving with blank eyes. His blood is pooling across the lino, almost touching my rubber soles.

I can see the living room and the Rifter from where I sit. It's stopped pulsating but I still long to be there, to finish what I started. Tears roll down onto my suit. Even as he lies there on the floor, I want to blame him. Why couldn't he have stayed away, just let me finish, see it out? I wipe the saliva from the corners of my mouth.

The grimness, the filth, the loneliness was all held at bay until this moment. The hope of a life beyond this, the glue holding my shattered spirit together. My thoughts are a haphazard jumble of memories. Chloe's baby fingers wrapped in mine, her small woven white blanket. I see her again, but as a toddler, a small Hello Kitty hair tie barely containing her mop of blonde curls. Her uncoordinated steps as she giggles, pushing her plastic dolly across the lino in a pink toy buggy bought from the charity shop. I imagine her as a woman, away from this place, someone new, living a world apart from here in an expensive leafy suburb, tall and smiling, looking like she belongs.

I close my eyes, not only from exhaustion but from the need to shut out the world. A cool gust of wind from the open window fills the flat and a rustling from the floor brings me back. Bits of rubbish from the fallen bin scatter across the kitchen floor. The wind filling the flat turns warmer, more humid. The wall in front of me illuminates with a white light, and I feel strangely drawn to it. I look to the window for its source, but all I can see is the same grey skyline beyond. The dripping from the tap has stopped.

The light from the wall suddenly fills the entire flat with a radiant warmth. I feel a sense of oneness; my body feels almost weightless. The world of Jerry, the Rifter, and my hopes for Chloe and our life together feel like they belong to someone else as I reach out toward the light. I squint, holding my hand up as a shield. Something is moving in that light. That is when I see them.

Bright letters hang, bouncing in midair— a familiar yellow haloed 'LEVEL 34' and then three options: PLAY, PAUSE, STOP.

Ishita Fernandes lives in North London, England. She creates near-future thrillers focused on the dark side of technology, science, and the impact on society. With over twenty years working in executive positions across some of the world's largest technology and consulting organisations, she draws upon her experiences as inspiration to create an immersive read. Ishita completed the Faber and Faber "Writing a Novel" course in 2020. Her first short story, "Static Road" has been published as part of the *Mixed Bag of Tricks* anthology and represents her sharp, dark, and visceral fiction. She is currently working on her debut novel.

Website: www.ishitafernandes.com
Facebook: @ Ishita-Fernandes-Writer
Instagram:@ishitafernandeswriter
Email: ishitafernandeswriter@gmail.com

UNNOTICED

By GESS

It is fascinating, for example, to compare how we remember not just specific events in our past but the more general feeling of an era. – Tyler Stovall

---

The so-called negotiations between The Little Country and The Imperialist Behemoth were of no consequence to the two young children at play in the bedroom. Growing up is hard enough to do without international, political, and economic *Sturm und Drang* about a matter they could not influence, even though it was sure to affect them. Where in the grand scheme of global enterprise did these young lives fit? In reality, the children knew nothing about the issues being reported, discussed, and analyzed by people around the globe, even their parents.

The discussions had been going on for years. The care and keeping of a great engineering wonder of the modern world was a serious business of global importance. The two governments argued about everything: management of the artificial waterway; governing of the districts around it; maintenance of the inequities implemented to support the segregated, elitist, and xenophobic systems that had worked for one administration so that they would perpetually benefit the other.

The meetings of dignitaries and the protests of civilians headed most of The Little Country's news broadcasts and front pages. Although little of the quotidian goings on like small-town elections and youth accomplishments were reported, life went on as usual for much of the citizenry. The morning buzz in the capital city had more to do with the uniformed children making their way to schools all across the city than with matters of national significance.

The major thoroughfare, Vía España, was abuzz from morning until nighttime. Personal cars were few, and taxis were even fewer. Most urbanites opted for the privately owned buses that ran sans schedule from as early and as late as the owner-driver wanted or could manage. The big, brightly painted *Chiva* buses seeped cumbia and merengue from open windows. The small, older *chivitas* were like rolling libraries in comparison; sedately painted in three stripes at most, quiet as old ladies praying rosaries at noon. And the raucous *diablos rojos* blared at the touch of a horn or custom button, The Grand Entrance trumpet fanfare best known from horse races at the Hipódromo Presidente Remón.

At the corner of Avenida Martin Luther King, in a short building with four residential stories, all manner of popular tunes flowed from apartment windows. In a corner apartment unit on the second floor, a young couple danced to Stevie Wonder's "Signed, Sealed, Delivered." They moved smoothly around the simply furnished living room, barely wrinkling their stylish shirts and slim creased pants. Their smiling brown faces reflected intermittently in the decorative mirrors on one wall. The record, a couple of years old, still played like new –due to their meticulous care.

In the bedroom, two children tossed a small springy ball back and forth across the bed. The children waited on their parents as patiently as a seven- and four-year-old could: they found a game to play. It was simply to get a small ball from one side of the room to the other.

The boy, Onorio, was gregarious and energetic. Already his teachers were struggling to keep his body in his seat and his attention on the lessons. Comparably, his little sister Imaculada was far more eager than she was capable. Their game wasn't evenly matched. But from her station in front of the bunkbed, Ima concentrated will and energy to keep up with the suitably named Super Ball, an excessively bouncy two-inch rubber ball. Onorio put little effort into lobbing the ball, aiming close to Ima's little hands. Sometimes it landed right in them, and he celebrated like he had scored a goal in the *Copa Mundial.*

Other times it bounced wildly, ricocheting off a wall or the tile floor, and Onorio paced the far side of the room while Ima chased down the toy. One of those times, the ball took a high hop off the smooth floor. It landed on the upper bunk of the stacked wooden bed. Before he made his way around the bed and across the room, Ima clambered up the ladder as she had seen him do many times before, quickly and without pause, like the sure-footed circus acrobats they had seen.

Ima was not allowed up there. That day, she demonstrated why that was.

Onorio was Ima's favorite and often only playmate. But the older he got, the more often he was lured out of the apartment by the other children in the building. Without her. So, she was eager to resume the ball game before their parents brought it to an end. In a flash, she'd climbed up to her brother's bed and retrieved the ball. To get down, she again mimicked her brother's skillful movements.

Onorio was a lanky boy, tall for his age and fearless. And the bed wasn't so high. Although there were only two or three ways to clamber up to the top bunk, there were hundreds of options to get down, each one swifter than the other. He'd developed a deft method of descent from the top bunk that treated the ladder like a slide rather than a series of steps. In position and with his height, he was more than halfway to the floor.

Ima, no doubt used to her brother's descents as though from the heavens, was a brand-new, first-time practitioner. She was the kind of little sister to follow him around and butt in on his games and copy what he did. Not only did Ima—younger and female—occupy the bottom bunk, but it had a guardrail to keep her from falling out of bed. In another year, Ima also would be "tall for her age" and later "tall for a girl," but not yet.

With the ball in hand, or clutched between her teeth, or tossed down below—neither child remembered later which and soon it would be completely irrelevant—Ima shimmied over to the ladder. Instead of turning around and stepping rung by rung, as she should've climbed, Ima made to "slide" down the ladder like her brother always did.

She purposely skipped the first rung. Then, she missed the rest of the ladder entirely.

It's not so dramatic as it sounds. There was her brother's face shining in the light of a sunbeam coming through the bedroom window, a moment of darkness, and then Onorio grimacing.

Ima's head met the tile with a sound so awful that the memory of it caused Onorio nausea for the rest of his life. "It's like nothing else I've ever heard." And that's saying something from the boy who grew up with a litany of tumbles, careens, sports injuries, and head traumas.

It was he who screamed, and he who cried first and loudest. For a few seconds, Ima lay stunned on the cool floor. She was getting herself into an unstable seated position when her parents ran into the room.

The ensuing minutes could only be described as "contained mayhem." Onorio's legs folded under him, and he plopped down. The mother blanched and rushed back out of the room. The father grabbed up Ima. Wide-eyed, he marveled at the *chichón* rising on her forehead. He called out for his wife to return with ice folded into a towel. With terse commands, he got the family organized, out the door, and into their car three stories below in the parking area tucked into the counter of the C-shaped building.

There was a trip to the hospital in the car Dad had at the time. Not to the nearest public hospital, but to The Imperialist Behemoth-owned-and-run health center. Its administration was more inclusive than their homeland and actually treated workers' children to the best of their capabilities. Immobilization. X-rays. Cognitive tests. The beginning of innumerable appointments for exams and EEGs. Luckily for Ima, she didn't need stitches and didn't develop scars. That was unless her brain had scarred in some then-undetected area.

Ima could never say what went wrong. How gravity pulled her down. What her head meeting the tile sounded like. Why she wasn't scared. "I must have blinked," she tells herself in later years, even though in her memory there's darkness for longer than it takes to blink before the tile floor rushes up to meet her.

For years, her subconscious tried to process the incident through a dream. It was less of a nightmare—since she never felt afraid—and more a peculiar memory that felt familiar but not right.

Ima finds herself sitting comfortably atop the low wall that borders the apartment balcony, the partition between safety and meters of open air above the ground. She looks down at the cement floor that extends out as a ledge. Below the ledge and Ima's dangling feet there is only darkness. It's night and dark in a way that signals a lack of streetlamps and moonlight. The commercial ground floor and first residential floor below are lost in the darkness. The field of overgrown vegetation and urban wildlife next door is darker than the night sky.

Ima leans forward and her stomach drops. Her head and torso lead the way, anticipating that the rest of her body will follow. And although she's facing away from the building, she falls backward into the black nothing. She is calm and unafraid despite never reaching bottom.

∽

EVERY MORNING AFTER, she woke with the feeling of remembering something forgotten; except, she's always known about the fall off the top bunk. What she knew without any doubt was that she wasn't supposed to be up there. And there was a lesson to learn from that.

The dream recurred for years. Not nightly or even frequently. She remembered in her tweens feeling curious about whether it was the same dream and, if so, what that meant. She remembered, too, trying to control it; to look up at the sky, or turn around and watch the ground, or climb back onto the balcony. It was a feat she never accomplished. Even now, the best "control" she has in dreams is to become aware that she's dreaming—usually during an incredibly frustrating dream—and wake herself.

Ima's fall quickly became legendary. Her grandparents used it to excuse pampering her. *Tías*, *tíos*, neighbors, and her mother's *comadres* told it to keep their own children from harm, real and imagined. But Ima thought of it little, except when the seizures came.

The first happened a month or two after the fall. As she later learned, she was at the dinner table with her parents and Onorio. She stopped speaking in the middle of animated chatter. Her fork slipped from between her fingers. She held her breath and stared, unseeing and unblinking, as the clock ticked loudly in the silence left by the family. Half a minute later, she blinked once, puckered up her face, and then resumed talking.

It happened again before they could take her to the pediatrician. And numerous times afterward. She'd just stop whatever she was doing and sit staring open-mouthed at nothing. She wouldn't hear people calling her name or feel them tugging her arm. It would last for a few seconds, thirty at most; then *Poof!* back to normal. Petit mal seizures are marked by this sudden brief lapse of awareness. Without witnessing this behavior, doctors were leery of diagnosing Ima with epilepsy or any other traumatic brain injury. The grand mal seizures served to clarify that matter.

Tonic-clonic seizures, as they're now called, have two distinct phases with a combination of symptoms. The tonic phase includes a generalized stiffening of the body, at times with skin discoloration caused by poor circulation or oxygenation that may lead to loss of consciousness. This phase may begin with a moan or cry caused by muscle spasms forcing air out of the lungs. It's followed by the clonic phase, a loss of consciousness and muscles spasms, then a period of sleepiness, confusion, or agitation.

Ima's seizures became the stuff of family lore, with repeated retellings of episodes by various family members. She could clearly envision, not from memory but by imagination, biting into Tío Ernesto's hand deep enough to draw blood during one episode. She felt bad about that since he was one of the uncles who died of sickle cell disease. He lived into his thirties, married, and fathered two sons who, like their many cousins, carried sickle cell trait but weren't afflicted with the disease.

WHAT FOLLOWED WERE years of seizure activity, doctor's appointments, scans, and medicines. Some episodes precipitated a rush to the hospital, like the first time, leading to overnight stays for observation. Each time, by morning Ima felt fine after a good sleep; quick to boredom and playing with other children in the pediatric ward.

The episodes continued until Ima's twelfth birthday. The last attack came during a school lunch period, unfortunately for Ima and her classmates. She was lunching on a meat-and-rice dish and grape Fanta soda. Though not always, this particular tonic-clonic seizure induced vomiting. Ima's friends at the table witnessed the reappearance of the purple-hued contents of her stomach. Luckily for the lunch staff, no one experienced sympathy vomiting in solidarity or disgust.

That last seizure is the only that Ima remembered with any clarity. Maybe because it happened at school and she was embarrassed, or she was getting older, and it wasn't so potent. Whatever the reason, she remembered the sticky mess on her uniform blouse, seeing through tears as she made her way to the infirmary, the nun nurse who advised her *"Tómate una siesta"* and then told *Papi* that she'd fainted, which Ima vehemently denied.

It brought a dramatic end to the seizures caused by Ima's fall off the bunkbed.

It is of course impossible and completely undesirable to separate personal lives and stories from broader historical narratives. —Tyler Stovall

---

In the tense climate of the laborious international negotiations, Ima's accident went largely unnoticed outside of her substantial extended family. The most public attention it got was a mention in the neighborhood church's next Sunday Mass when parishioners were asked to pray for specific afflicted members of the congregation.

It remained one of Ima's earliest childhood memories, right along with following her brother about. There is a particular photo in the old family album that Ima remembered often. At the bottom of the white instant print photo frame someone has penciled: 1971. A brown boy of about five years of age, with thick-rimmed black glasses and a big smile, wearing an under-shirt, belted slacks, shiny dress shoes. A two-year-old girl toddles close behind him, drinking from a bottle. A couple of her ribboned plaits are in mid swing. She wears a diaper, frilly white bobby socks, and orthopedic brown boots. Soon, the boy will sport a pressed button-down shirt and the girl an equally frilly dress.

Wherever the boy went, the girl followed. Always. They're passing the walnut brown door of an open closet in a bedroom with teal walls and a bunkbed accessorized to safeguard Ima and her line-up of dolls from falls and other harms from the convulsions. The apartment was where they lived, but that bedroom was home. Where Ima imagined the interior of the other apartments she never saw. Where she played with her yellow terrycloth baby doll on the steps outside their door, pedaled her tricycle up and down the hallway, and ran amok with other children who lived in the building.

The apartment was refuge, too, from the terrifying *diablitos* who harassed passersby for days before Carnival. She liked skip-ping along to the bus stop, hand in hand with her mother so she wouldn't wander into the street, to ride the party buses to down-town. At twelve and taking bus rides by herself, if she lucked to catch her uncle's bus, he gave her change *from* the fare box instead of having her put any in. For decades, the Grand Entrance trumpet call remained one of Ima's favorite tunes. It took her back to being a little girl in a cool apartment in the capital city of a little country full of music.

When Ima was seven, the two governments reached an agreement. The three-quarter-century animosities between The Little Country and The Imperialist Behemoth fully resolved with a pair of treaties named after the representative Colonel and President in 1977, from which all everyone ever focused on was the line about the termination of The Imperialist Behemoth's control at noon of December 31, 1999. The new treaty superseded the previous 74-year-old one.

The streets are loud still, but only with honking. Public transportation was gentrified in the new century, with light-rail trains pairing with patriotically painted buses that run on schedules. There is one passing in the online VR photography images of the street in front of the apartment building. And sometimes, in The Imperialist Behemoth city where Ima lives now, she hears The Grand Entrance trumpet fanfare bleating from a lowrider and smiles.

GESS WRITES stories about women thriving in life and in love. She holds University of Washington BAs in English and Spanish Literature and a MA Degree in Latin American Literature from the University of Texas at Austin. GESS was the winner of the 2020 Yellow Bird Editors First Page contest and a finalist in the 2015 Writers' League of Texas Manuscript Contest (Romance category). She's a member of Contemporary Romance Writers, Inclusive Romance Project, Texas Romance Writers, Women's Fiction Writers Association, the Writers' League of Texas, and the long-running Pen and Fork writing group. She makes her home in Austin, TX. Learn more about her at http://www.writtengesstures.com/

THE ACHING STORM

By E.A. Williams

The first humans to step foot on Ryva did not respect the planet on which they had landed. They were, like so many other explorers from the ninth quadrant: hungry. Ravenous for money, for adventure, and worst of all, for glory. These first humans were sent from the resource acquisition arm of Apex Industries.

In the dry season, when the rivers are at their lowest, fossilized pieces of old Apex mining equipment can still be seen peeking up over the water's surface.

The second humans were the rescue team Apex Industries sent to retrieve its personnel, though it was rumored they were there to finish the job the first team could not. At the time, the company was not ready to give up on the prospect of a planet as large as Ryva: full of precious minerals and positioned, as it was, ninth planet from its twin blue stars, almost exactly halfway between the two largest colonies in human-occupied space.

It took twenty-seven years for the first sapling to breach the hull of their transport ship where it now sits, the old Apex Industries logo peeking out from beneath sacred vines, faded in color, but not in memory.

The third-wave humans never met the first two. They were not prospectors or rescuers; they were not even colonists, though by default that is what they would become. It was a mistake that led the Demi Terranna to land on the surface of Ryva. Specifically, a mistake in the engine, built by Apex Industries, to carry four thousand and twelve people from Ohio II to the farthest colony planet in the quadrant, Duce Rome. *Landed* is too gentle a term to describe how the Demi Terranna slammed into the canopy of a dense cusp of trees in the mountains, where it is still lodged to this day.

The ship is a temple to the Seven Waters now, a place of worship and education for those dutiful enough to receive its gifts.

It is from those survivors-turned-colonists, brought to Ryva by a faulty combustion cap that nearly cost them their lives, that the planet came to be inhabited by humans. And should anyone, be them Ryvinian or not, forget that Ryva is not a planet to be trifled with, the Seven Waters remind them.

One for cleansing, one for life, one is always giving, and one made of strife, there are two be they sisters that meet in cold, the last is a stranger you meet when you are old.

Yasha twisted the links of her mother's chain tighter into her palm and waited for the weight in her chest to ease. When it did not, she looked up into the canopy of the great Mauchai trees that formed the city of Twaug. A hovercraft zipper past, filled with gawking tourists from some other human colony, all of them already waterlogged from the endless Ryvinian mists. They were likely headed to the famous waterfalls: a must-see stop for any well-traveled human in this part of the galaxy.

Yasha had been off-planet in her youth; her mother had insisted upon it. She had refused to let Yasha even study at the temple until she had been to at least three of the other colonies in the sector, which Yasha had begrudgingly visited with the other daughters of the temple priestesses. At the space port, her mother had held Yasha's face in her palms, the calluses on her fingertips brushing aside homesick tears Yasha was already fighting and said, "Trust the current; it always finds its way."

Her mother had been right. No matter how she railed against it, Yasha's current had found its way. When she turned sixteen, she practically ran away to the temple school to study to become a priestess of the Seven Waters, as her mother had before her. On the day of Yasha's confirmation, her mother stood tall and proud, her long black hair glistening with streaks of grey against her white robes, as she called Yasha's name for the temple of Vek. Again, her mother had held her face in her palms. This time it was her mother who had cried. The weight in Yasha's chest bobbed dangerously with her memories.

It was supposed to be an honor to spend the last year of her apprenticeship sequestered in the halls of the high temple. She wished she had never gone. She wondered if her mother had known she was ill when she said goodbye to Yasha then.

When her father had seen her off, at the start of her Aching

Storm, he had pressed his forehead to hers and promised it would get easier. But her grief had landed in the branches of her heart with no more grace than the Demi Terranna, and with no promise of rescue. Her father promised though that the weight in her chest would settle, that the journey would make her strong enough to bear it. But her father mourned her mother for almost a year before Yasha had even left the seclusion of her apprenticeship in the high temple.

Guilt had been peeking through the twisting vines of Yasha's grief since she had come home to find her mother gone. Her father had buried her in their grove alone. He had undertaken his Aching Storm alone. And now Yasha was taking her journey of grief to the sunken temple of Tarsheir alone.

She touched her hand to her chest, tangling her mother's chain with Yasha's matching one, a confirmation gift from her mother. They were beautiful pieces, twisting silver made to mimic the sacred weir berry vines that grew everywhere from the mountain temple of Vek to the sunken city of Tarsheir. A soft pitter-patter began above her, and Yasha knew without checking her comms-glass that the day was in its fourth cycle. It was only the second rain of the day, and it would rain again before the dual suns set. The rain brought with it the fruity smell of the weir berry and the audible gasps of the tourists as they stuck out their tongues to catch the sweet rain that poured from the sky every day. Clutching both chains close to her heart, Yasha closed her eyes and tilted her head back to revel in the rains of Ryva.

Water washed over her toes, lapping up her ankles as the tide of sweet rain rushed down from the foothills of Twaug and through the roots of the massive trees that made up the city. The clouds were heavy with rain this year, and so the weir vines were heavy with fruit—a good thing for the temples and the tourists, but a burden for the bustling shops nestled in the many branches of the tree city that had to halt business to clean their homes from the sticky residue it left behind. Blessings were funny like that.

A shout from a branch above startled Yasha. She opened her eyes just in time to see a burly man in climbing boots falling shoulders first into the rising flood waters. Her cool gaze met his panicked one briefly before he tumbled past her. Another tourist. With a hefty sigh, Yasha gathered up the long skirt of her robes and waded into the still-building currents.

To his credit, the man wasn't flailing wildly or grabbing at passersby as he slid down the embankment. He bumped into several knobby roots before Yasha could get ahold of his shirt collar. She tried not to judge him too harshly—the waters of Ryva were quite deceptive in their tranquility. It wasn't his fault he did not know residue from the sweet rains tended to build on the lower branches and the slippery smooth walkways were better negotiated barefooted. Yasha dragged the man up the soft embankment of roots, carefully digging her toes into the moss and rock with nimble precision, until she could lean him against one of the massive tree trunks.

"Silly tourists! Always slipping in the rain," a sister from the local bowery admonished lightly. Yasha recognized her by her green and purple robes as she rushed over. "I'll take him, sister," she told Yasha. "Wouldn't want to sully your white linens.

Yasha's white robes marked her as a sister of the mountain temples. It was an honor she shared with her mother, and one Yasha had not gotten used to. A stain of cerulean bled down from the knees of her linens. The pollen of the weir bloom, like the blue wine the Seven Sisters made from its berries, was permanent.

What was another stain? she thought, as the man she'd rescued began coughing. Her robes were beginning to feel more like a canvas already.

"I won't worry about it if you won't," Yasha said with a smile, trying to shake off the dizzying feeling of her grief bobbing in her chest. "Besides, I think they need you more than I do at the moment."

Yasha nodded to the small group of little faces peering over the railing from the branch above them where the sister had come from. Memories of the classes her mother taught floated unbidden to the surface of her mind. The hypnotic sway of her mother's silver chain as she read the old Earth stories to the children; the way her mother's eyes twinkled when she came to her favorite part, she would look for Yasha and wink.

They were memories Yasha treasured and resented; she forced them down. "We cannot stand to lose even a single one of our teachers, not even for a moment. Otherwise, they might ask me to teach the little ones, and no one wants that."

"If . . . if you're sure." The other woman looked between Yasha and the man, then up to the sets of blinking eyes that watched them.

"I am sure, sister." Yasha used the informal address with a warm heart. It was not a little thing to feel the support of family, even in a stranger's kindness.

"Then I will go tend to my wayward flock." The woman bowed her head slightly, as was customary between the sisters of the Seven Waters. "May your storm be brief."

Yasha frowned, wondering how she had known Yasha was in mourning. Then she remembered the blue length of silk tied around her ankle, visible now that she had come to the tourist's rescue. Shaking off another wave of unwelcome melancholy, Yasha bowed to the teacher and turned back to her new charge.

He was still coughing, as unsteady leaning against the tree trunk as she had been flying her first hovercraft. She suspected this situation would be going about as well as that one had. At least he was right side up. As she stood over him, wondering how long she would need to tend to his hacking fit before the oath of her station would be satisfied, a fuzzy little deenk climbed out of his pocket, its round ears folded flat to its head.

Deenks had the misfortune of being both prey and pest on Ryva. The tiny round creatures had surprisingly strong back legs and long fingers they used to climb. Their tails were twice as long as their bodies and covered in the same dense green fur, which led many tourists to think they were huge caterpillars instead of harmless marsupials. Many deenks had fallen victim to the squealing, swatting hysteria of tourist season. So, Yasha was surprised to see a usually skittish deenk cozying up to this half-drowned tourist. The man started in on another round of coughing, his chest folding over his knees to shake the last of the water out of his lungs, and the deenk jumped onto Yasha's chest, climbed up her silver weir berry chain, and nestled right under her thick braid of black hair.

"Well, aren't you a charming surprise?" Yasha asked the little creature as she reached up to give it a pet. The deenk chirped back happily.

"He is that." The raspy voice of the nearly drowned tourist reached her. "I'm Leith." He grunted, pulling off one of his ridiculous boots with a heave of effort. "Leith Struan, and that is Derek."

"Derek?" Yasha asked, the animal's long fingers wrapping

around hers as she pulled her hand away. "How very Terran of you. So, I guess you are not a tourist?"

"Tourist? Why . . ." Leith looked down at his boots. "Right. No, just a biologist, I'm afraid."

"Well then, you should know better." She admonished him with a rather pitiful huff of exasperation.

"Yes, I should," Leith sighed, peeling off his socks. "I am afraid that I am not quite my studious self just now."

One of his grey soggy socks squelched off, giving Yasha a glimpse of a knotted length of blue silk ribbon around his ankle that matched her own. She was beginning to see the work of the Seven Waters here and wished for a moment that she couldn't.

"You are in your storm," she said softly.

"You know, I used to think it was a funny thing to call grieving a storm." Leith poured water out of one of his boots and looked up at her. "Especially with all the other words out there to use. Thought maybe it was just a part of the whole water worship here. The people of Ryva do name a lot of things after water.

"That we do." A smile tugged at the corner of her lips, threatening the pall that had hung over her mood since beginning this journey three weeks ago.

"I get it now," Leith ducked his head, speaking to the ground at her feet. "The Aching Storm, it's kind of poetic."

"One for cleansing, one for life, one is always giving, and one made of strife, there are two be they sisters that meet in cold, the last is a stranger you meet when you are old." Yasha barely realized she was humming the old rhyme before she had already finished it.

"I've always hated poetry." Leith sighed.

"I have found most scientists do." Yasha smiled again, a sad one this time, tinged with sympathy.

Derek the deenk took that moment to spring from his perch on her shoulder and land on Leith's head with a small indignant squeak.

"I know, little guy." Leith gently plucked Derek from his forehead, holding him up to look the tiny creature in the eye and apologize. "I am sorry, you know. Wasn't thinking."

As if he could understand, Derek chirped back rather disgruntledly but unfolded his ears. The motion rounded out his already rotund face. He reached out with grasping fingers toward Leith, and Yasha noticed that one of his paws didn't open all the way.

"He's hurt." Yasha didn't know why, but the idea made her want to cry.

"He was hurt," Leith responded, looking from Derek to Yasha. "Careless botanist stepped on him some time ago when I first arrived on planet. Couldn't leave the little guy like that, so here we are."

"Most people think they're pests." Yasha knelt to stroke the deenk's dense fur. "But they pollinate the weir vines; without them, the berries wouldn't grow. In a way, they saved the first Ryvians from starvation. Our little pests and our little saviors."

"They are deceptively important." Leith's eyes paused on the blue silk knot at her ankle. "I thought I had met a sister from every order, but your robes are foreign to me."

"I'm Yasha." She shrugged, standing up and offering him a hand. "I came from the mountains."

"Where they make the wine." He nodded. "It makes sense you understand these guys then.

He tucked Derek into his front pocket before taking her

hand and following Yasha up the embankment and back onto the path toward Tarsheir.

"Are you—" Leith said awkwardly, passing his boots from one hand to the other. "Are you going to the sunken temple? I don't want to intrude—I just . . ."

"I am going." Yasha answered before he finished, the weight in her chest as heavy as it had ever been. She changed the subject, starting along the path, assured that he was competent enough to follow or at least not drown. "Did you know deenks are patrons of the Seven Waters?"

"Really?" Leith accepted the implied invitation to follow her.

"Yes," she said and smiled over her shoulder, catching sight of Derek peeking his round black eyes over the cuff of Leith's pocket. "It's why the spas can't spray for them, and why the tourists get such a heavy fine when they step on them."

"They really should be more careful." Leith returned her smile. "The tourists, I mean."

"I thought so," she answered.

They fell into a quiet rhythm after that. Occasionally Leith would point to a coratt swinging from branches overhead or a flock of taughty birds and explain some strange part of their anatomy or mating habits.

"Their wings have webbing between their feathers," he explained excitedly. "At first biologists thought this was entirely a function of their semi-aquatic lifestyle, but then Dr. Marcus Shurber observed a nesting pair communally preening each other's webbing before mating."

"I didn't know." Yasha answered him perfunctorily, letting his voice roll over her like thunder.

He even stopped once to show her a mushroom growing on the side of a tree trunk, which, he exuberantly explained to her, was a bearded threshelle mushroom, only found on Ryva and one that could, if taken in small doses, induce extremely vivid dreams. In large doses, the threshelle caused compulsive itching, bouts of involuntary arm movements, and the belief in the person who had consumed the fungi that they had become invisible.

Yasha didn't mind the interruptions, and, if pressed, might have even admitted to liking the company. The distractions kept her mood lighter than it had been in weeks. For once she felt as if she could breathe.

The woven branch paths of the city led them from one massive tree to another, winding beside the river. In the rainy season, the roots of the Mauchai trees wouldn't be visible under the river's current. The walkway forked, east and south, where the river split into many smaller streams. This too would be hidden in the rainy season, when the river ran in one path, in all directions. They took the southern path toward the cliffs and Twaug's famous waterfalls. It sloped up, gently at first, and then more aggressively, until even Leith had to quit speaking so he could focus on his breathing.

It was nearly dark as they finally made it to the spa. Run by the green-robed sisters of Twaug, the spa crested the steep cliffs, denoting the end of the city. The cliff-top sanctuary was one of the few places on the whole of Ryva where anyone could see over the giant trees. The canopy swayed with the breeze, and Yasha could hear the roar of the waterfalls as they tumbled over the cliff's edge below. The artificial glow of the city couldn't touch the dark of the forest. In the overwhelming evidence of her smallness, Yasha found relief. The sisters at the spa would give them shelter tonight. It was their duty, as it was the duty of every priestess to comfort those in their storm.

"Thank you," Leith said as they reached the spa's entrance. He fidgeted with the boots in his hand. "I know I talk a lot. Andy was always saying that I could talk your ear off if you let me. So . . . thank you."

"You have said a lot today." Yasha turned to smile at him, stopping short of the entrance. "Was Andy . . ."

She trailed off, letting the pitter-patter of the sixth-cycle rain finish her question for her.

"Andy was my wife, or she was going to be my wife." He sucked in a great lungful of air before continuing. "She was studying records in Maubyeta when we met. I was only supposed to be on planet for six months."

"You stayed longer?"

"I would've stayed forever." There was a hitch in Leith's voice, a half-choking little hiccup. "When my fellowship ended, I applied to stay on Ryva permanently."

"Is that when?" Yasha looked at her hands, unable to look at his grief any longer. It was such a private thing, so like her own.

"No," Leith almost laughed. "I followed her to every library and archive on the planet for two years. And then one day she was gone."

"She left?" Yasha frowned, her own sadness reaching out to his.

"No." Leith swallowed down some unknowable emotion before explaining. "There was a tourist, drunk and shouting about the rain. I couldn't reach her before they fell."

The sadness in Yasha's chest turned sharp.

"I was in seclusion when my mother passed." Yasha offered up something of her own story, a link between their grief. She looked down at the silver chain wrapped around her wrist. "This was hers."

Holding out her hand, Yasha let Leith run his fingers over the delicate thorns and berries that made up the links of her mother's chain.

"It's beautiful." Leith's hand was warm against her arm, and when he pulled away, she felt cold.

"My mother made them both." Yasha touched the matching chain around her neck. "The sisterhood encourages us to become craftsmen. Art is evolution and prosperity, a tangible way to express our relationship with the divine."

"And here I thought all you priestesses just made wine." Leith quietly huffed.

"We do that, too." Shifting the heavy folds of her robes aside, Yasha pulled out a neo-leather wineskin from her side. She took a swig. Offering him the sack, she watched a group of tourists just inside the entrance, swaying nearer. Leith's warm calloused fingers brushed her own, jarring her out of her muddy thoughts as he took the wine she offered.

Leith sighed, a heavy breath that slumped his shoulders and saw him lean defeatedly against the branch opposite her. This was part of the Aching Storm; this weighted nostalgic melancholy that surprised Yasha in quiet moments that had dominated so much of her journey already. As she watched him sip from the wineskin awkwardly, dribbling a not-inconsiderable amount of the dark blue liquid down the front of his shirt, Yasha considered that their tides were meant to meet.

"Thank you," Leith said, stretching his arm across the doorway.

As Yasha reached out for her wineskin, there was a triumphant shout from one of the swaying tourists just inside the spa. The low sizzling sound of someone breaching the eco-barrier that kept the rain and bugs outside of the spa's lobby barely registered in her ears before a man, tall and bulky, wearing shoes and one of the spa's fluffy green robes, stumbled out. His meaty fingers snatched the wineskin out of her palm. A priestess in a green robe bustled after the drunk man, a tight smile on her face.

"Mr. Fletcher," the sister began, frustration clear in her voice. "That is not your property."

The man spun around. His sleeve caught on a thorny link of the chain around Yasha's wrist. He stumbled, and his drunken weight pulled them both off balance. Yasha's hands tangled between the man's oversized sleeves as he flailed, attempting to right himself. Yasha felt her feet slip out from under her. The path was now dark, and all Yasha could make out as they tumbled out of the spa's light was the blue-tinged lips of the man as he warbled a surprised curse. His boots fought to find purchase on the slick walkways.

They rolled almost to the edge, where the dark path gave way to the cliffs the spa overlooked. Yasha wrenched one of her hands free from the tourist's grasp, desperate to stop herself, and found Leith's warm palm.

With their free fall now at a stop, a shrill chaos exploded out of the eco-barrier of the lobby as the man's fellow tourists realized their friend was not coming back with more wine, and that required further examination.

They found him lying on the ground, inches from falling into the darkened abyss and they howled with laughter. Leith's grip on Yasha's arm tightened at the sound. He lifted her to her feet and Yasha looked into his rugged face to see his jaw clinching. His eyes tracked the group's movements with a predatory swiftness. The boisterous group hoisted their compatriot up with enough huffing and slipping that Yasha was worried they would all be sent sliding over the edge, but no. As they moved past, Leith hugged her tight against him, putting his body between Yasha and the drunk who nearly knocked her off the cliff.

Leith was shaking as he watched the tourists waddle jaggedly back into the lobby, no worse for wear. Yasha couldn't tell if Leith was angry or afraid. She didn't know whether or not she was either of those things. All she recognized at the moment was that she was standing on a cliff, in the dark, with the roar of the waterfall filling up the space between her breaths.

One for cleansing, one for life, one is always giving, and one made of strife, there are two be they sisters that meet in cold, the last is a stranger you meet when you are old.

When they returned to the light of the spa's entrance, Yasha took stock of the splotches of blue weir berry wine and mud that now coated her once pristine white robe. The robe she had missed her mother's last words for. The robe that had cost her a year of goodbyes. The robe that marked her as a Priestess to each of the Seven Waters, a position worthy of envy, and one she had already grown to despise.

They had looked better on her mother.

There was an image seared in Yasha's memory, of her mother standing alone at the top of the high temple's steps, her robes white, her body looking tall and strong. Tears shimmering in her eyes as she watched Yasha go into seclusion. It was Yasha's last memory of her mother. It was barely more than a year old; time Yasha could have spent with her.

A consuming anger boiled in her chest, threatening to spill out from her throat as her hands went numb, and the blue length of silk at her ankle felt like a shackle. Tears sprung up in her eyes, and Yasha looked up to the heavens, praying that Ryva would bless her with a cleansing rain. Ryva was silent, save for the roar of the waterfall.

A gasping sob wracked her body, buckling her knees. Before she could crash back onto the ground, Leith gathered her up, wrapping his arms around her as her body shook with the force of her cries. He rocked gently back and forth as her tears soaked his shirt. Her arms went numb from being trapped between his.

Finally, the tears stopped, and Yasha pressed her palms against Leith's chest, giving herself a chance to catch her breath. The light from the spa's lobby barely reached them, but as she took a shaking breath, Derek the deenk poked his head out of Leith's pocket, his huge round eyes catching silver in the light. She rubbed the tiny creature behind the ears, his presence a welcome distraction, until it wasn't. Her wrist was bare; her mother's chain was gone.

Spinning around, Yasha looked out at the inky darkness that shrouded all but the faint circle of light coming from the spa's lobby.

Even if it were light, she thought. There were so many cracks and slippery crevasses where her mother's chain could have fallen. She would never find it now. The last part of her mother was gone, and once again she didn't get to say goodbye.

"It's gone," Yasha whispered. To acknowledge the loss to Leith, to Ryva, if only so that she might begin whatever new stage of grief this put her in.

"What's gone?" Leith's soft sturdy voice wavered.

Yasha turned to face him, clutching the remaining weir vine

chain, tears welling in her eyes. His eyes flashed immediately to her empty wrist, and she knew she didn't need to say anything. Leith knew. Leith had come to her knowing. It was the way of the waters to bring all that was needed with the current.

With a deep breath to steady herself, Yasha walked back to the entrance of the spa. The sisters of Twaug would give them shelter for the night, and in the morning Yasha and Leith would follow the cliffs down to the sunken temple of Tarsheir, where they might, waters willing, end their journey.

A BEEPING from the bedside drew Yasha out of her trance. The morning was grey. The cliffs of Twaug were covered in an early mist hanging low in the trees that dared to grow down the steep slope. The mists were unusually heavy even for the class seven water planet. Looking out, Yasha could imagine herself standing above the clouds with only the sound of Twaug's famous waterfalls to ground her.

The night had been long and, in many ways, harder than even the first night of her journey. The beeping came again: three clear tones in quick succession. She sat stiffly on the edge of her bed, watching the faint blue dots of Ryva's twin stars finally crest the canopy as the mist settled over the leaves. She blinked back fresh tears. Her father had promised she would be strong enough to carry this hurt, and yet here she was. She wondered if her father was a liar or if she was weak. Her comms-glass beeped insistently, letting her know the morning had come. Wiping her face free of tears, Yasha stood—willing, if not ready—to face the storm.

The lobby served as a waystation of sorts for those visiting

Twaug: tourists and priestesses alike. Ryva, for all of its beautiful features, was known for its waterfalls and its wine, and the sisters of Twaug had a monopoly on both. Stepping into the lobby, Yasha felt an unexpected jolt of anxiety shoot through her chest.

Where was Leith? She thought. *Had he left without her? They hadn't made plans or promises.*

Looking over the throng of people, most human and some sporting the green robes of the sisters, Yasha searched for him. When she spotted Derek from his perch on Leith's shoulder, the deenk began chirping delightedly. Only then did Leith look up from the table he was bent over. His mouth was tight with concentration, his bushy unkept brows drawn together, giving him a disgruntled look that suited him.

Letting up a prayer of thanks to the rain for bringing their storms together, she moved her hand to press her mother's chain to her own before a black empty recollection claimed her. *I will never hold my mother's chain again.*

Before she opened her eyes, Leith put his arm around her, his voice low and strong.

"It will pass," he said. The certainty in his voice almost made Yasha believe him. "Come on, I got you something to eat."

He guided her to a low table with four comfortable-looking poofs arranged around it. Two of them were laden with Leith's boots and jacket, a makeshift sign of possession in crowded rooms. As they approached, Derek took a flying leap from Leith's shoulder, landing on the table with a squeal of indignation. The tourist couple who had been edging their way closer to their mourning nest flinched, backing away without a word. The deenk looked back at Leith and Yasha triumphantly before hopping his way across the table and claiming a dish of weir berries for his own.

"I worry that he's shy," Leith said, with a grin on his face that suited him just as well as the frown had.

"I can see why," Yasha murmured. She smiled; her affection for them both overpowered her sorrow. "Thank you for the breakfast."

Nudging Leith's jacket out of the way, she sat gingerly on the poof. All the parts of her body that were made to bend had stiffened through the night and ached now with exhaustion.

"Don't thank me yet," Leith groaned as he lowered himself into the seat, rolling his shoulders and neck until something popped, and he let out a sigh of apparent relief. "I can't really take credit for the food. Sister Tibby got it for me. The coffee is probably cold. It's been a while."

"I don't mind." Yasha picked up the cup of coffee and took a sip. It wasn't really hot or cold, and it wasn't really coffee. Coffee beans wouldn't grow on Ryva, and even if they did, the Common Bonds and Boundaries Treaty of thirty-one-thirty-four prevented anyone from calling it coffee if it wasn't grown on Earth, but Yasha didn't mention that and reached instead for a pastry.

"So, um, while you eat, I wanted to give you this." As he spoke, Leith's voice wavered. "It's not perfect. It was broken pretty bad, and I didn't find it all in the dark. I'm not sure it would have made a difference if it were light out, but I did what I could. It's—here—it's better than nothing."

Leith thrust his arm out stiffly, his large hand fisted around something. The rambling and uncomfortable look on his face made Yasha put down her breakfast. He shook his hand at her;

whatever he was holding jingled softly, and she held out her own hand in response.

Her mother's chain fell into her palm in a lump.

"You found it." Yasha stared at the clump of silver, not blinking, worried that if she did it would vanish.

"Most of it." Leith nodded, drawing his arms back as he clenched and unclenched his fists. "It was really dark. We can look for the rest of it today. I talked to Sister Tibby already and she is happy to give us shelter for another night before we go to Tarsheir. And if it takes more than that we can—"

"No." Yasha cut him off. She grabbed his hand, a tremulous smile on her lips. "Thank you, so much. I do not know what words could convey the care you have shown me, but the storm has to run its course."

"Even if you aren't ready?" Leith looked down at her hand where it clasped his own, and she knew by the threat of tears in his voice that they weren't speaking about her journey.

"Anyone who is ready to weather this is a liar." Tears dripped down Yasha's nose and she ignored them.

"I've always been a terrible liar," Leith gasped, tears of his own falling down his cheeks.

"But an excellent friend." Yasha sucked in a breath, scooting her poof closer to Leith's so she could lean her shoulder against his.

They stayed like that for a while, leaning on one another, the noise of the crowd ebbing and flowing.

THE MIST HAD GIVEN way to the late morning when they finally departed, several of the sisters draping them with strings of the red haorth flower, as was custom for the sisters of Twaug.

It was another reminder to her that she was not alone. Yasha curled her mother's chain around her wrist, the once fine links twisted in the spots where Leith had mended it. This was not his craft, and it didn't need to be. Yasha felt the care all the same.

The path down the cliffside was twisting and narrow, marked by an ancient handrail made of the scavenged parts of mining equipment left behind when Apex Industries abandoned the planet a thousand years ago. The first real settlers of Ryva had made good use of the company's leftovers.

Derek hopped from Leith's arm to the calcified banister that kept hikers from slipping into the green forest abyss at the bottom of their climb. The deenk trailed beside them as Leith and Yasha slowly hiked down the path. They only stopped when passing behind the great waterfall. The weir vines parting around the rocks dangled in delicate strings of green leaves and blue flowers.

Standing under the jutting rock that protected them from the pouring water, Yasha paused, utterly surrounded by the rush of water and the sweet smell of weir berries. The roar was unimaginable. It bombarded the senses until everything was silent, overwhelmed by the power of the water. Her breath slowed as the smell of wet earth and cold rock filled her nose. The mist of the falls drowned out the heat of exertion, and in the shadow of the water's power, she was small and her guilt even smaller.

Yasha stopped to look out into the water. This is what made Ryva special, what protected it from being strip-mined for all of its precious minerals, what brought it life and death. It was in the waters that Ryva found its creation and destruction, and it was here that Yasha always found herself. It was where she would find her mother's spirit when she needed her.

"SHHHH, *all will be well, my love." Her mother's words overtook Yasha. She was four again and her mother was pulling her from the sister rivers that intertwined below their home. Yasha's teeth chattered as her mother held her to her chest, wrapping Yasha in her thick white robes. Her mother stroked her cheek, rocking her back and forth. "Careful my love, the water is strong, and the current always finds its way."*

WITH A LONG EXHALE, Yasha turned back to the path, her robes heavy with the mists of the falls. Leith held out his hand, his eyes soft and unfocused as he looked just behind her to the water. She took it, squeezing his fingers in a gentle reminder that he was not alone.

As they neared the bottom of the steep cliff path, a sheet of icy water covered the ground, getting deeper with every step. The stone quickly gave way to mud and roots as the pair ventured into the Sunken Forest of Tarsheir that spent half its life under water. Tarsheir sat over a massive rhodium deposit, one of many on Ryva, and the only to have ever been mined. The basin was, in part, a result of the disastrous mining expedition Apex Industries sent. Their explosives had carved the lowlands down to the bedrock, and their crew built steel and concrete structures in the wasteland they had made, a place for miners to sleep and eat between shifts in the tunnels. But like most things on Ryva, the water took it back.

As they walked toward the temple, they were joined by

others: a procession of mourners taking advantage of the low tide to end their storm in the river's temple.

The farther they walked into the forest, the darker it became. From the ground, the trees blocked out the twin stars and the only light came from bioluminescent fungi that grew out of the roots and branches of the trees. Occasionally a botsluang bird, its belly glowing orange and red, would swoop past, croaking its low song through the wilderness. Each time they passed, Leith stopped and gawked in wonder while Yasha smiled.

The water was at their waist and their feet numb with cold by the time they could hear the hum of the temple's song.

A gentle golden glow reached out from the temple's entrance, beckoning the weary mourners closer. The temple itself was nearly invisible in the dense jungle of trees and vines, but the entrance rose tall between two ancient trunks, vines heavy with leaves and berries twisting between the stone and trees. Two plinths stood on either side of the entrance, flames wafting skyward in defiance of the rain.

Reaching into her bag, Yasha pulled out a dried length of weir vine, thick enough to stand straight and dipped in paraffin on one end. She turned to Leith, ready to offer him the torch she had carried all the way from the high temple, only to find him ready with one of his own. She should have known. Leith may not have been ready for the storm, but he was prepared for the journey.

They lit their torches on the plinths as they walked into the temple; the heat of the large flames briefly warming their skin as they passed. As they neared the heart of the complex, humming grew into the wailing song of the temple's priestesses. Leith nudged Yasha with his arm, pointing to a tunnel high on the temple wall, where one of the sisters of Tarsheir stood in her blue hooded robe, her face obscured by a thin veil as she sang. They passed more tunnels and more sisters, the haunting song echoing off the calcified walls and washing over Yasha and Leith like the roar of the waterfall.

"They're welcoming us," Yasha whispered to Lieth, and even that echoed.

They walked close together, following the other mourners and the gentle current of the river's low tide. Leith and Yasha found themselves in a cavernous room. Here, the stone temple had been eroded by the whims of the river's current, and patches of the ground rose above the water nearer the walls and at the very center of the room. Looking up, Yasha saw more tunnel openings with blue-robed sisters standing watch, singing their woeful melody.

Yasha took Leith's hand again, her mother's mended chain biting into both of their palms, leading him toward the altar in the center of the room. Stepping out of the water, Yasha felt for the first time in hours the weight of her sodden robes. Her faith was heavy now, and even as her robes dried that wouldn't change. But she would. This is what her father meant.

"Fighting the current doesn't make you strong, my love." The memory of her mother's voice was soft. *"It only makes you tired."*

They reached the long stone table that stretched from one end of the altar to the other where a group of sisters, each with a long needle and thick ball of blue thread, sat crocheting a tapestry of blue silk ribbons.

"They spin the thread from the old tapestries when the tide comes in," Yasha explained to Leith as they watched. "The marker of our storm is made from the storms of the past, and so ours will make the future. In this way, we are all made one in the waters of Ryva."

"What if I am not ready to let her go?" Leith didn't take his eyes off the gossamer weft of silk as each blue ribbon took its place in the picture of grief before them.

"I don't think we are letting them go," Yasha murmured.

"I—I—" Leith's voice quavered. He turned to look at Yasha, tears already falling down his cheeks. "I don't think I can."

"Then we won't." Yasha hugged him tight.

"You should." His voice was muffled against her shoulder. "You've come all this way."

"Shhh." Yasha hushed him, leaning back to wipe at his cheeks with her thumbs. "I didn't get here alone."

"But," Leith gulped, taking a steadying breath.

Yasha put up her hand to stop his protests.

"Let's sit for a while." She led them to an empty patch of ground and sat.

The cold water lapped at their toes, and Yasha reached for her belt, bringing out her half-full wineskin and taking a sip. Basking in the strange peace of the echoing chamber, she offered the wine to Leith, who took it reluctantly.

"I'm not tough enough for this," Leith said, taking a long draw from the wineskin.

"None of us are." She looked back up to the altar where a dozen more people were placing their blue ribbons on the table for the sisters. "Wouldn't it be awful if we were?"

"I—I—" Leith paused, his thought suspended in the ineffable design of the storm. "What am I supposed to do if I am not —if this is over? What if I lose her after? What if I lose the love she gave me?"

"I don't know." Yasha shivered, the cold finally getting to

her. "I think if you look for her in the places that you found your love for her, she will be there, and so will her love. But I know they aren't in here."

She looked around the chamber. Tears fell down Leith's chin, mingling with the cold waters of the river, and Yasha had to blink furiously to stave off her own wave of tears. It was useless as they crested anyway, sending the cavern into a kaleidoscope of fuzzy blue and gold shapes.

"You're starting to sound like a poet," Leith said with a watery laugh.

"I'll try to keep from rhyming." Yasha wiped her eyes with the back of her wrist.

"See that you do." Leith brought his knees up to his chest, wrapping his arms around them. Derek gave a little squeak, climbing out of Leith's breast pocket and into his hair. Leith let out a huff of laughter, reaching up to give the little creature a gentle scratch. "Where would I even start looking for her?"

Yasha smiled, folding her arms around her own knees.

"In every library and archive on the planet if you have to." She laid her cheek against her knee so she could look at him. "Didn't you say you would have followed her forever?"

"But what if I'm not strong enough?" Leith looked out at the water.

"I didn't think I was strong enough to make it here." She sighed, turning her head to rest her chin on her knees and look out at the water. "I was wrong. Maybe you are wrong about this."

"Yeah, but I am a scientist," he said, his tone flat. "And you're practically a poet."

Yasha looked back at him, to see a playful smirk trying to wipe away the pain on Leith's face.

"I know you're right." Leith's voice went soft, barely audible over the lullaby of the blue sisters. "But I'm scared."

"So am I." Yasha reached out her hand, and he took it, squeezing her fingers tightly before letting go.

The knot was difficult to undo. It had been tied for a long time, and the water made it tighter with each storm weathered and river traversed. They sat at the water's edge in the den of the sisters' haunting melody, working their knots undone, until the grip of the pale silk released.

"Oh." Yasha nearly gasped. It felt like an eternity, pulling and tugging loose the loops of her grief, and now it lay on the stone floor, ready to become a part of the next storm. Leith made a noise beside her, and she knew his knot was undone.

Together they stood limply, at a loss for words, the water lapping at their feet. Together they carried their ribbons to the altar, and together they watched as a blue-robed sister picked them up, ready to add them to the new storm.

One for cleansing, one for life, one is always giving, and one made of strife, there are two be they sisters that meet in cold, the last is a stranger you meet when you are old.

E.A. WILLIAMS IS a graduate of the University of North Texas, where she studied film and playwriting. While completing her degree, she stretched her creative limits helping to run a writer's collective, as well as studying special effects. Her love for the fantastical can be seen in her thrilling debut series *The Line of Tepes*, which invites readers to explore Williams' hometown of Houston through the lens of a sexy vampire noir.

Tiktok: @eawilliamsbook
Instagram: @e.a.williamsbooks
Website: www.eawilliamsbooks.com

THESE BOOTS. OR THE BITCHES OF EASTWICK

By Roanna Flowers

No one asked what kind of liquid accumulated along the intersections of Sixth Street in downtown Austin. Everyone—locals and tourists alike—resolved within themselves to call it condensation, the result of a day's worth of soaking humidity that gave everything, including the brick and concrete of that old street, a luminescence.

The sheen of what everyone agreed to call condensation turned the city street and its uneven curbs pink with the glow of a now nightly phenomenon—girls traveling arm-in-arm while wearing an assortment of glowing pink penis beacons.

They had become a peculiar plague to the modern-day city. While people scared and distracted themselves with any number of potential and cinematic apocalypses, they missed the bachelorette tourism that had consumed their streets, their famous intersections, and their day spas. Bars that had been sanctuaries were reduced to playthings for packs of pending brides. Murals that had once entertained or beguiled shoppers and drivers passing by now had reservation spots on mobile apps. Each bit of street art had its own eddies of young women caught at invisible turnstiles, each waiting their turn to make a wish and capture the perfect angle, perfect moment, perfect picture of the final days of a single life.

It was a waking funeral—celebrating the death of Waiting and Hoping and the entry into the only heaven that really mattered in America: the creation of a wedding registry.

It was Friday night, or more accurately Saturday morning, and multiple lines of sashaying, swerving, stumbling chorus girls of impending marriage and lifelong happiness were turned loose from the bars that had attempted to contain (and entertain) them. They veered toward ill-advised car rides with men they just met for parties they just heard about. They swerved toward anxious Uber and Lyft mobiles. They tumbled into one of many prearranged party buses that were parked along the side streets that fed into the Sixth Street party artery.

Stragglers fell victim to tip-preying pedicabs. And for one unfortunate horse named Zelda—whose name was bedazzled against a custom-made crown encircled by a halo of bats on springs from Party City—two of the matrimonial horde clambered their way onto the phantom limb that was her carriage attachment with a shrill peal of laughter. It was no way to end an evening. She never wanted to be clip-clopping down Sixth Street in the first place. It was horse hell for a past infraction she could not imagine having committed. She shook her head at the indignity of it all, sending her personal swarm of bats in all directions.

HIGH KICKING off of the curb at the corner of Sixth and Congress, wearing pink Steve Madden knee-high cowboy boots and dressed in white mini dresses of varying styles, hems, and expense, a group of eleven women spilled into the street. All White, they looked as if they were designed and built in the same White-woman factory with the same spray-on tan and pressed-to-perfection blonde hair, each donning a similar white satin sash with pink glitter lettering that declared them 100% Horny, 100% Drunk, and 100% That Bitch.

The one in the middle of her carbon-copy companions wore a sash that read 100% His Bride. Arm in arm, they made a phalanx, unbreakable by any oncoming pedestrian, pedicab peddler, or Lyft driver. They chorus-line high-kicked onto Sixth Street with the final burst of remaining bodily coordination only to fall into one another's glittery, perfumed arms.

It was like watching the last call of butterflies flitting into the street and into the fading memory of a hangover.

The collapse of the phalanx turned into a group hug. Sticky air clung to their golden hair long ago made flat by the clinging sweat of hours-long dancing. They pressed painted lips on cheeks, leaving butterfly pink smudges behind, and the group of eleven peeled off one by one, dwindling down to a group of three remainders: 100% That Bitch, 100% His Bride, and 100% Drunk.

"100% Drunk" (real name Emma Beauchamp, bridesmaid, and Capricorn) flipped her hair back and threw up her last vodka cranberry to the stumbling squeals of her remaining two friends, the ones she called The Real Ones.

Rounding the intersection, its slow roll kept barely at one mile per hour due to the flash flood of inebriated humanity forgetting to follow any of the street safety rules learned in kindergarten. A dark sedan came to a stop, its headlights beaming against the white dresses, glitter bedazzled skin, and pink glittery sashes, turning the three women into human disco balls. The passenger side window lowered halfway, enough for the word "Bethany?" to issue out of it.

"Yes!" the three of them cheered, arms raised, underwear visible beneath the harsh beams of the headlights. Laughing, they piled into one another and then into the back of the black C-Class Mercedes. The driver watched the image of them in his rearview mirror as they formed a group hug in the backseat, none of them capable of buckling up for safety.

The city's lights reflected on their faces—young and full of freshly graduated excitement, with new lives about to be led— butterflies whose wings were still wet.

Bethany "100% His Bride" Mueller was going from home to sorority house to married life as the wife of Jordan Nesmith, a meteorically successful financial investment executive in his late twenties, a recent University of Texas alum and Delta Sigma Pi man. They were going to stay in Austin, it was decided, with frequent business-class trips to New York. Their plan: he would become the next Warren Buffett, and she would save the world one cocktail party at a time. She was going to become a partner of The Firm—that was the fun little nickname Jordan had given their soon-to-be marriage.

Ashleigh "100% That Bitch" Campbell wore the blinking pink penis circlet denoting her as maid of honor or a modern fertility goddess. Like Bethany, she had decided to stay in Austin (with weekly trips in first class to New York), in the condominium on Rainey Street that her parents had purchased for her as a starter home after graduating with honors in Marketing and a minor in TV-film. She was already TikTok famous, with over two million followers taking her advice on everything from artisanal incense to the latest in sustainable brands, and she would soon come to a television and smart-phone screen near you as the "What's New Wednesday" influ-encer anchor for *Good Morning America.*

Emma Beauchamp—still 100% Drunk even after donating her last vodka cocktail to the sheen of Sixth Street—would be leaving her sorority house for an L.A. loft. Her future was wide open, and her plane ticket was already tucked into her Apple Wallet, waiting to be scanned.

Having an eleven-person bridal party was considered osten-tatious even by modern, Southern standards, but with Emma leaving for L.A. and Bethany leaving singlehood, the wedding would be the last time they would all be together.

They didn't notice the frequency of the driver's eyes appearing in his rearview mirror. He grabbed glimpses of their interlocked arms. He glanced at their pink-booted spray-tanned legs, each one crossed. His eyes took extensive notes about where the glitter had decided to accumulate with the sticky sweat of their night spent dancing. His point-by-point inspec-tion was illuminated by the blinking pink light of a novelty penis. He even noticed the horse carriage using him as a cattle guard to move through traffic, its driver dressed in layers of black despite—or to spite—the night belonging to a humid Austin June.

The driver slowed to a slow-rolling crawl from one narrow

street to another. His eyes prowled the numbers on the buildings in search of an address. The bars that crowded the condos (or was it the other way around) were closed. Any throngs of drunks they had released upon that narrow strip of street had already disappeared. The street was naked, without even stray threads of drunken tourists to cover it.

"Oh my god, drive faster," Emma complained, not at all concerned about her Uber rating—she wouldn't be living in this town much longer. She won't have to care. She'll be driving everywhere like everyone else in L.A., complaining about the traffic.

"Shh!" Ashleigh and Bethany filled the backseat of the car with their eighty-proof shushing. The driver glanced up to the rearview mirror.

"Don't shush me," Emma said, and the three women sputtered into laughing.

"He's going to give you a three," Bethany said, cracking up and into the arms of her best friends, sorority sisters, and bridesmaids.

"I've never been anything less than a ten," Emma said, giving the driver a wink as he looked back in the mirror.

Catching the wink like a blown kiss, the driver smiled—his smile discernable only by the creasing of his eyelids in the reflection of his attention. Emma felt her vodka cranberries coming back to haunt her in the pit of her stomach and the back of her throat.

The Rainey—cleverly named—was a 34-story complex with an infinity pool, floating gardens that reimagined the greenspace that was once there when Driskell and Rainey carved up this part of the city for themselves, and enviable views of the river (that the city's inhabitants insisted on calling a lake—which also had two separate names that no one could agree on). The covered drive that valets used for customers clamoring to visit the on-trend establishments up and down the narrow slice of urban exclusivity was dark, the lounge above was closed, and the valets were long gone. It had the air of deluxe abandonment. The car pulled in and came to a stop.

Their arms and legs untangled, and manicured hand reached for manicured hand as Emma opened the right-rear passenger door. The driver's eyes trailed after each one of them. "Have a nice night," he said. He leaned close to the steering wheel to watch them, one by one, slip into the lobby, the head-lamps of his car lighting their way. Only once they were safely inside did he pull away.

He gave them a five-star rating for not throwing up inside the vehicle, even though he was going to be finding glitter in his car for a year.

Arms linked again—an old sorority trick to keep from falling down while inebriated—they piled into the elevator, laughing. Their arms released once they were able to use the walls of the elevator for additional, luxurious support. Steepling their finger-tips together and touching thumb to thumb, they formed a three-layered triangle and looked into one another's eyes. The blinking pink penis filled the elevator with a heartbeat-pulsing glow. "Let us love-love-love one another-other-other to the end-end-end," they chanted full voice, the elevator's acoustics ampli-fying their sorority song, "of time-time-time!"

Hands and thumbs pressed tight, each one to the other, they closed their eyes as the elevator continued to climb. "Delta three! Delta tri! I will be one till I die!"

The elevator stopped at the top floor. The doors opened and steepled hands turned to interlinking fingers, creating an unbreakable chain as they boot-scooted into the tastefully appointed elevator foyer, with its glass and gold tables between the two sets of elevator bays, each with a spotlight highlighting the work of a local artist and a dried flower arrangement with its painted cockleburs and pink-and-white pampas grass.

"Shhh!" they all told one another, and then giggled at the simultaneous nature of their own warning.

Ashleigh's graduation present was a three-bedroom, three-bath, three-thousand-square-foot penthouse apartment with clean, uninterrupted spaces, hardwood flooring, and floor-to-ceiling windows that provided a glorious view of Ladybird Lake, known as Town Lake by old timers and the Lower Colorado River by geographers, geologists, and certain pedants who would take pains to remind everyone in earshot that the "lake" was actually the result of the damming of said river.

The open floorplan dazzled with its immediate, high-priced view and easy access to the kitchen just to the right, and the wide expanse of a white living room straight ahead.

Once the door closed and they were no longer in danger of pissing off the HOA with their noise after midnight, they steepled their hands again, and pressed their thumbs together to make their triple-layered triangle from kitchen to living room.

"Delta three! Delta tri! I will be one till I die!" They chanted in theatrical whispers, trying to be quiet while ultimately failing at it.

"Delta three! Delta tri! I will be one till I die!" They shimmied their way to the sectional sofa, their path lit in pink by the blinking penis beacon, their hands and bond unbroken.

"Delta three! Delta tri! I will be one till I die!"

A static shock, created perhaps by the friction of glitter between their pressing hands and the jostling of their dancing, ran up their spines, zapping between them in a three-way circuit. Trapped in the triangle they made, it bound their hands, forcing togetherness. Their shared circuit transformed into a bolt that silenced their chanting with a final triple gasp, shook their bodies, and frizzed their hair.

WHO ARE YOU AND WHY HAVE YOU DISTURBED ME?

The voice knocked them back, each to a separate spot on the sectional that they then clung onto like a life raft. Pink light pulsed against the walls and revealed the outline of a hulking figure. It was fortunate the living room had twenty-foot ceilings; the creature needed a good seventeen feet for clearance. As it was, his iguana-like spikes and bat-like wings had to be uncomfortably tucked in to avoid scraping the ceiling and breaking the glass. He looked a little like Godzilla in the face, something about the jawline, and also—in the right light, at just the right angle—Jon Hamm.

Damn the HOA; they screamed. Bethany was in incoherent tears, Ashleigh was shocked into indeterminable, open-mouthed terror, and Emma shouted: "Who are you?"

WHO ARE YOU?

"You answer first!" Emma demanded.

YOU CALLED ME!

"We didn't call you!" Emma snapped back.

I CAN ONLY COME IF CALLED.

"Well, that must make you really popular with the ladies!" Emma said. "Or men. Or lizards. I don't want to assume your situation—"

I'M PANSEXUAL.

"Well, good for you—!"

IT IS GOOD FOR ME. IT'S VERY GOOD—

"So, what do we do now?" Emma said. "Make a wish? Bethany! Stop crying!"

Bethany tried to swallow her sobs, repeating "I don't want to make a wish" like a yoga mantra over and over again.

I DON'T GRANT WISHES.

"Well," Emma said, and she climbed up to stand on the thick sofa cushion, increasing her height from five-foot-seven to eight-foot-seven, or monster chest level. Making yourself big worked against bears—maybe it would work against whatever the hell this was. "We called you here—you said so yourself. Now you have to do what we say!"

THEY'RE NOT MY THING—

Emma folded her arms across her chest. "You have to. We're your masters now."

The monster intruder folded his own arms against his five-foot wide chest, his bat wings scratching against the sheetrock.

NO WISHES! IT'S NOT WHAT I DO. I DON'T DO WISHES, GIVE ADVICE, OR MAKE DREAMS COME TRUE!

"What *do* you do?" Ashleigh's voice popped up from behind a sofa cushion. While Emma had distracted the whatever-it-was and Bethany was hyperventilating to keep from screaming, Ashleigh had created something of a pillow fort in the corner of the sofa. It was not a formidable defense, but it made her feel better. The monster stood as tall and as broad as he could without breaking the window or getting himself tangled in the macrame planter that hung in the corner. The iguana-like spikes that lined his spine from the tip of his tail—the end of which was somewhere near her kitchen island—stood on end.

MY NAME IS MIGHTY FURFUR, THE GREAT EARL OF HELL—

"Ohmygod ohmygod ohmygod," Bethany said, rocking forward and back, her arms hugged around her body.

"Shitshitshit," Ashleigh said behind her makeshift pillow fort.

"What do you want?" Emma's courage would serve her well in L.A.

Furfur sighed, covering his scaly face with his left claw.

IS ANYONE GETTING MARRIED IN THE NEXT WEEK?

"Yes! She is!" Ashleigh piped up from behind the pillow, and she and Emma both pointed to Bethany.

"Shut up! He's going to sacrifice me like a virgin," she hush-shouted that last part to Emma, as if he couldn't hear it.

"You're not a virgin," Emma stage-whispered back. "You're as safe as the rest of us—"

AND DID YOU CHANT THREE PHRASES OF INTENSE, PERSONAL MEANING TO YOU WHILE FORMING A TRIANGLE?

"Yes," the three of them said, Ashleigh's voice muffled by upholstery.

THEN,

Furfur said, as he folded his bat wings in an official pose around his body,

AS YOU HAVE SUMMONED ME HERE ACCORDING TO THE SACRED REQUIREMENTS AND RITUAL— MORE OR LESS—I AM OBLIGATED TO TELL YOU THE TRUTH.

"The truth," Emma said, looking to her two best friends, The Real Ones, the ones who had locked arms since rush week. Ashleigh opened the pillow door to her fort and stared at her. Emma spun around to face the monster. "Is Jordan—"

"Emma," Ashleigh piped up, "don't—"

"—having an affair?"

YES.

"I knew it!" Emma shouted.

"WHAT?" Bethany cried. "I'm getting married in a week!" Her despair, with the aid of vodka and tequila shots, crystallized swiftly, passing multiple layers of psychological evolution in nanoseconds, from that starting anguish to poised purpose and couched anger. "Who is Jordan cheating with?"

ASHLEIGH. AND THE CHECKOUT GIRL WITH THE NOSE PIERCING WHO WORKS AT THE H-E-B AT MUELLER.

"That bitch!" Ashleigh and Bethany looked at one another as both shouted the same thing at the same time—directed, of course, at different people.

Emma plopped down on the sofa, bouncing as she laughed out: "I knew it. No one needs to go to H-E-B that much."

"It's not funny!" Bethany shouted at Emma.

"How could you!" Ashleigh also shouted at Emma.

"How could *you*?" Bethany turned on Ashleigh, her gaze stabbing in repeated accusation.

"Right? You were supposed to be *a Real One!*"

At Emma's couched accusation—soaked in passive-aggressive, holier-than-thou judgment—Ashleigh tossed aside her fort cushions and climbed up on her feet to a stand on a neighboring pillow. "Did Emma get her workout gear and shoes from a Nike influencer deal?"

NO. SHE BOUGHT THEM WITH MONEY SHE EARNED AS AN INSTACART SHOPPER.

"You bitch!" Emma said.

"How many followers does Ashleigh actually have?" Bethany climbed up on her own two feet to stand on the sofa.

5,000 GENUINE FOLLOWERS. SHE HAS MAXXED OUT A CREDIT CARD BUYING THE OTHER TWO MILLION.

"Ha!" said Emma.

"Does Emma have a job with Universal Studios?" Ashleigh volleyed back.

YES—

"Ha!" Emma said again.

SHE IS A TOUR GUIDE—

"Ha!" Ashleigh barked back to Emma. "We're walking, we're walking, we're walking, and we're stopping!" Ashleigh threw up her hand, flat of her palm extended in the international sign for *Stop* and also, for a brief time in the 1990s and perpetuated on Nick at Nite reruns, *Talk to The Hand*.

"I'm breaking into the business as a PA," Emma said. "I have to gig for a while, so what? At least I'm not blowing my best friend's future husband in a bathroom!"

AT A PLUCKERS—

"No one asked you!" all three of them shouted.

Bethany's psychological evolution finally carried her to

courage, and she turned to finally truly look at the monster in the living room—the one who wasn't her maid of honor. "When did Ashleigh and Jordan first betray me?"

IN THE BATHROOM ON THE NIGHT OF YOUR BIRTHDAY PARTY AT ONO'S—

"My birthday party?!" Wobbling on the cushion like a barely functioning toddler, Bethany raised her arms. "So, do you only screw my fiancé at big life events?"

NO. SHE ALSO SEES HIM ON REGULAR TUESDAYS.

"Gym day?" Bethany said, astonished at the additional betrayal of their weekly fitness goals.

IF GYM IS SHORT FOR GOT YOUR MAN, THEN YES.

Emma struggled for balance as she made her way back to her feet and drunkenly crossed the sofa cushions like they were hot coals at a corporate retreat fire walk. "Come to L.A. with me, Beth—"

SHE NEEDS HELP PAYING THE RENT—

"No one asked you!" all three of them said again.

I AM ALLOWED TO PROVIDE ADDITIONAL COMMENTARY AT MY OWN DISCRETION.

Bethany closed her eyes—mistake!—she opened her eyes

again to stop the room from spinning and shook her head, which was also a mistake. Nausea gathered in her throat. "No. I can't. I'm getting married in a week—"

YOU CAN'T BE SERIOUS.

"Come with me, Beth," Emma said again, holding out her hand. "Does it mean we could get a better, bigger place closer to the city? Yes."

An actual truth from a friend hit the air like a gong, and Bethany took her friend's offered hand. The two of them steadied one another. "I've always wanted to learn how to surf." Both hands joined together, turning into a tight hug that sealed their friendship.

Ashleigh's pink penis beacon pulsed to a steady rhythm, something close to an average human resting heartrate. It created a tom-tom to the building seconds of Ashleigh's increasing FOMO. After seven beats, Ashleigh stood, this time on her own two feet on the throw rug that covered the hardwood floor. "Bethany: I'm sorry—"

THAT'S ONLY HALF TRUE.

"No one asked you!" all three of them shouted.

As the last joined sound of their voices raised in unanimity ended in their commingled breath, the demon in the corner disappeared. Ashleigh stripped off her maid of honor penis crown and crawled into the arms of her friends. They hugged in glitter and terror and tears, mumbling: "I'm sorry, I'm sorry, I'm sorry . . ."

In the pulsing pink glow of the penis crown that lay

tumbled on the floor, a small figurine of a bat—a replica of the *Nightwing* statue at the corner of South Congress and Barton Springs—cast its shadow in the corner. And in the hush of a deserted Rainey Street, the clip-clopping of a world-weary horse finally getting to go home echoed off the condos, reflections of her swarming bats flying against the wood and glass and stone.

Roanna Flowers is a comedy writer in Austin, Texas. Raised on Mel Brooks, Monty Python, and Bugs Bunny, she listened to stand-up comedy albums while other kids were listening to Disney soundtracks. She was once picked Most Likely to Be a Stand-up Comic by her First Grade homeroom teacher. Her last comedy short film appeared in over 30 festivals worldwide, including the Cannes Short Film Corner. You can see her short film work on www.roannaflowers.com and find her elsewhere via linktr.ee/roannaflowers. Roanna is currently querying her first comedic novel and writing her second.

THE RULES OF SABERTOOTH SANCTUARY

By N.J. Knight

Rule No. 1: You must immediately sign the accidental death and dismemberment insurance policy. If you choose not to do so at this time, stop reading immediately, inform your appointed advisor, and take the next shuttle back to the dock. You will be compensated for your travel and time.

At the top of the world, Cassie experienced a frisson of fear and a pang of anxiety in her chest as she processed that rule, clutching the hefty silver pen with her suddenly cold fingers as she sat at the conference table. She was so close to her dream—working alongside Dr. Henry Blair himself—with only this mountain of unsigned documents in her way. Looking back, she wondered if the stark warning was listed first in order to weed out the cautious, newly minted high school graduates from those who were simply filled to bursting with ambition and excitement and pride.

This was Sabertooth Sanctuary, after all. The one place on Earth where aspiring zoologists from all over the globe could study with Dr. Blair, the preeminent expert on the most exotic wildlife the planet had yet sustained. He looked like David Attenborough and acted like a secret, unhinged Wild Kratts brother. Five-year-old Cassie had thought he was Santa Claus.

And so the obsession began. An obsession that rivalled fellow intern Taz's preoccupation with reviving the Tasmanian tiger he had lovingly named himself after.

"What college do I attend to become Dr. Henry Blair?"

"I'm having a grapefruit and granola for breakfast, just like Dr. Blair."

"I want the glasses that look like Dr. Blair's."

"Next summer, can we visit every National Park that Dr. Blair mentioned in his 2011 PBS special?"

She even dressed up like him for her third-grade living history project, and of course she included the video evidence in her Sanctuary application.

As an aspiring scientist, whether your interest was in conservation, deep-sea creatures, or one of the many species humans had pushed to extinction that now only existed on this small collection of islands in the middle of the Arctic Ocean, this internship was your one shot at becoming even a footnote in the annals of modern zoological history.

Naturally, the application process had been . . . arduous. But the onboarding was just bizarre, starting with the series of flights aboard smaller and smaller aircraft before a final, bone-chilling trip on the Sanctuary's vessel, the SS *Stellers*, to this very first rule. Cassie lightly stroked the embossed Institute letterhead as she processed the words. A golden-eyed sabertooth tiger stared at her from a field of silphium, Julius Caesar's favorite herb. Both brought back from extinction by Dr. Blair.

"Get a load of all these nerds. Scared of a little wildlife?" Not recognizing the vaguely Eastern European lilt, Cassie turned to see a smug blond boy lounging over the heated leather armchair to her left. The boy she later learned was Novák, whose parents owned a wildlife preserve also known as half of Madagascar's surviving tamarind forest.

"I don't know what you mean," she responded stiffly, pushing her tortoiseshell glasses up her long nose before signing all the waivers spread in front of her on the matte black conference table. It was time to meet her hero.

She remembered that seed of fear weeks later, watching two of *them* fighting over the pieces that used to be Novák's body. If she had left when they first landed at Fossey Station, the most disturbing thing she would have witnessed this summer might have been her best friend Sammy drunkenly vomiting all over the backseat of her mom's ancient hatchback.

Now, shivering with fear and cold and exhaustion, she tried to remember the interns who read the rules and waivers before deciding to begin the long trek back to a world that wasn't trying to kill them. But she hadn't even looked up. She was too excited about her dream job with her hero on the other side of the world.

Ten interns arrived for orientation at Sabertooth Sanctuary, but only seven boarded the craft that would take them to Irwin, the next research station on their journey.

They didn't know yet. They didn't *know*.

Rule No. 2: *Outside specimens, as well as electronic devices, are not permitted at the Sanctuary. This includes food and drink that could introduce contaminants to the lab environment. Leave all banned items in your assigned locker, and provide an itemized list below to your appointed advisor. Your belongings—or their monetary equivalent—will be returned to you at the end of your six-week internship.*

BANG BANG BANG BANG BANG BANG BANG

The intermittent, wall-shaking rapping at the barricaded emergency exit doors had shattered their sleep for almost three hours now. This time, one of the interns stirred.

"Go to sleep. It's just the wind," Cassie murmured. "Just the wind."

Soo-Young, only half-awake, seemed satisfied at Cassie's soothing tone, if not her words. She closed her dark eyes, head falling back as her breathing became deep and even once more.

"Just the wind," Cassie repeated, once more, for herself, fiddling with her glasses in the half-dark.

They'd been holed up in the Sanctuary's theater for two days now. The stale popcorn and comfortable reclining seats made it better than most other locations they'd found at Irwin Station. The soundproofing made it almost ideal.

But being designed for complete darkness with multiple entry and exit points they needed to chain shut every night? That made it very, very dangerous.

Nothing they'd tried so far stopped the creatures, though

daylight seemed to deter them. The bright glare of the midday sun at the height of the arctic summer was the only thing that had so far. Cassie wondered what the Sanctuary had done to stir these nocturnal monsters when they should be at their weakest. She imagined the predators would be crawling all over the island at summer's end in a few short weeks when night returned to the Arctic Circle.

At arrival, Cassie had merely been grateful for the ever-present summer sun that ensured the Sanctuary never became burning cold, only uncomfortably chilly. Now that most of the buildings on the island had lost power, the sun's perpetual hazy blue twilight had become essential to their survival.

Not for the first time, Cassie imagined herself lazing on sticky plastic loungers poolside with Sammy, pop music blaring from a nearby phone, plausibly deniably alcoholic drinks sweating in water bottles on the concrete ground beside them as children shriek-screamed through a game of Marco Polo in the water. A summer where sunshine was an annoyance to guard against with sunscreen and floppy hats, instead of a lifeline to deter horse-sized crustaceans who'd taken a liking to eating interns.

She glanced down at the cracked Spider-man watch on her wrist, a gag gift from Sammy currently kept taut with a short bungee Cassie had scavenged from a listing locker door days ago.

"You're *such* a Peter Parker," her friend had explained, ignoring Cassie's complaints as Sammy strapped it to her wrist. "Too much science in your head, and not enough common sense."

"You weren't complaining when I figured out how to make your sister's fish glow in the dark for Halloween," Cassie shot back good-naturedly, already admiring the red-and-blue plastic novelty on her arm.

"Most of them even survived," Sammy smirked.

"Hey! There's no trial—"

"—without error! Yeah, yeah." Sammy finished Dr. Blair's—and therefore Cassie's—famous tagline, rubbing the back of her shaved head in surrender. "Just lemme know before you start injecting weird DNA into yourself, OK?"

Cassie had almost lost the ridiculous watch when a particularly nasty tumble to escape a monster's grasping foreclaws that had cracked the watch face and half the cheap plastic band. Her fellow interns were nearly as frantic, though for less nostalgic reasons. The watch's lack of an Internet connection had become a lifesaver, as everyone else's Apple watches, mobile phones, and other connected devices had been confiscated when they arrived. Determining the exact time—and therefore how high the sun was—before venturing outside had become vital to their survival.

Three more hours till noon. Three more hours until it would be safe to open the door.

BANG BANG BANG BANG BANG BANG BANG BANG BANG BANG BANG BANG BANG

The long, interlocking segments of the theater's rolling steel door bulged and flexed, looking entirely too flimsy to Cassie's frightened eyes. Much more so than the padlock and chains that kept it closed tight to the elements and *everything else* outside. What if the creatures shattered it? What if they sliced through the interlocking metal with their opposable claws, serrated like a crab's, but so much larger, stronger, scarier . . .

"It's just the wind."

"Just the wind." She said aloud to the shuddering door itself now.

Rule No. 3: *Nothing you experience on this island can be disseminated without the express written permission of the Sabertooth Sanctuary and Dr. Henry Blair, in perpetuity. Decades of untainted scientific research depend on your cooperation. Violators will be prosecuted.*

None of them knew exactly where the creatures came from, or why.

They were unknown to the scientific community, as far as the huddled survivors could determine. Hell, even cryptozoologists hadn't imagined them. This batch of interns didn't have a carcinologist among them, and only one now-absent advisor— Benny, whose major personality traits were not answering questions and being from Alaska—had ever been close to the nearly barren Arctic Circle before the illustrious invitation to the Sanctuary.

Had Dr. Blair found the creatures frozen in the melting permafrost? Or were they always there, under the waves of the rapidly heating Arctic Ocean, driven to the surface by a lack of food or oxygen?

"I wonder if they hunt like Siberian tigers," Soo-Young had mused with Cassie, huddled together one sleepless fuzzy night that would soon bleed into blinding daylight. "Solitary, or mothers with their offspring?"

"So perhaps they're territorial, as well?" Cassie agreed, after thinking a beat. This was familiar logic she could understand, more so than trying to determine which labyrinthine half-formed trail cutting through the rocky terrain would lead to the docks where they might find a boat to escape this nightmare. Or even where their next meal would come from.

"That would explain why we weren't overrun immediately. And the scratch marks we've seen on buildings could be used to ward off potential competition for resources."

Soo-Young hummed in agreement, twisting her long brown-black hair up into a neat bun with her silver Sabertooth Sanctuary pen, a habit that had brought the two interns together earlier in the summer.

Before the coveted internship had turned into a survivalist bloodbath.

"It's our best hypothesis. For now, anyway. If only the CCTV were operational. We're losing *so much data*." Her soft, lilting voice touched on Cassie's own heartache. They were all in mortal danger, and they couldn't even document it properly.

Unlike Soo-Young's laser focus on endangered apex predators, Cassie's own scientific interests were more attuned to animal intelligence than one specific classification or biome, and in a normal world she would have been absolutely fascinated by these human-sized predators. They hunted in packs; communicated and plotted strategies with one another; they even seemed to use crudely made tools to create the chaos the interns were currently experiencing. They may not be on the level of Kea parrots or some species of cephalopods, but their behaviors were *fascinating* . . . as long as you ignored the blood-smeared floors the current survivors had been sleeping on the past few weeks.

But even the advisors who could have determined anything, like a weakness or even a genus, were gone now. Eaten or drowned or maybe watching them all die from behind the safety of a television screen. Cassie wouldn't put any of those options off the table entirely; survival of the fittest wasn't just an evolutionary theorem at the Sanctuary, but an overriding methodology if you were to prove yourself here.

That's why she didn't entirely blame the advisors for saving themselves—if they were alive at all.

If there were a CCTV, there'd be plenty of evidence of the beasts' feeding, sleeping, mating, and molting habits by now. She could imagine her erstwhile supervisors watching this horror story play out like a nature documentary, clucking their tongues at the latest intern brought down. *There's no trial without error*, after all.

Cassie pushed down the insidious fear that perhaps the Sabertooth Sanctuary had *created* rather than discovered these creatures. That way lies madness—specifically Novák's, before he was eaten. They'd all scoffed at his warnings about the Sanctuary's possible culpability then, but his words became less fantastical as their situation became more dire.

Which begged the question: If they could figure out how to capture the creatures, would that earn the interns a byline on the study, or disqualify them entirely for tainting the experiment?

Would the footage be shared in the name of scientific progress? A bunch of teenagers slaughtered by the chittering, skittering armored beasts, inscrutable eye stalks turned toward the flickering screens that showcased their own carnage, live on the airwaves in gushing, Technicolor crimson and stark bone white, for the entire world to see?

Maybe it would be the most-watched video in history. If there were anyone left to watch it.

Cassie imagined the public's response: *When Crabs Attack!*

Of course, if recent history were any indication, no one with any real power to stop the monsters would listen, anyway. They were too busy fighting their personal enemies: other countries, other religions, other humans who thought or looked or lived differently.

Bombastic old men would yell about the deviants running around in crab costumes menacing the ladies' restroom, while running B-reel of cheesy black-and-white movies from sixty years ago, plastic and foam crumbling off long-dead actors.

This idea was in sharp contrast to the hope surrounding Dr. Blair's mission that Cassie had fully invested in: bringing life back, after centuries of humans poisoning and ravaging the world, stealing resources, and killing the competition in an endless, mindless pursuit of whatever it was the world's top fifty corporations wanted. Sabertooth Sanctuary resuscitated lives snuffed out by human greed, and that's the purpose little Cassie had been desperate to latch on to.

Thump thump BANG thump thump thump . . . thump . . . thump . . .

This time it sounded almost apologetic, entreating. The wind didn't mean to alarm, you see.

It just wanted *in*.

Rule No. 4: *Respect your colleagues. For the safety of you and your fellow interns, it is imperative that you heed your appointed advisor. Sabertooth Sanctuary is an isolated outpost, and without utmost discipline, lab and field conditions can destabilize at any time.*

Although Cassie knew logically that they had been here a scant three weeks, she couldn't even remember what life was like before the emergency protocols had been initiated that shut down the entire fifty-mile radius around Irwin Station. She vaguely remembered taking food and shelter and *safety* for granted back then. Being warm. Joy and anxiety at meeting her hero, instead of her current exhaustion and despondency.

As the underaged Chilean uber genius of the group, Vicente, liked to remind them, they were *supposed* to be at the Darwin Station by this point in the program, exploring the science, ethics, and behaviors of reintroducing extinct species to their native biomes with Dr. Blair himself.

"What's he like?" Taz had once queried Benny eagerly in his heavy Kiwi accent, eyes bright with excitement in his burnished brown face. "Dr. Blair, that is. How does he approach the animals? Does he have a favorite to work with?"

Cassie, pretending to be as cool as the arctic evening, sidled closer to listen in. It had been a week since they'd arrived at the first stop in the Sanctuary tour, the Fossey Conservation Station, and there was still no sign of the man, the myth, the Oscar-winning documentarian.

Benny glanced up at them from behind messy brown bangs, and Cassie could almost see him trying to remember the teens' names before deciding it wasn't actually necessary.

"He's very, very busy," Benny finally deigned to respond before riffling through the pages on his metal clipboard. "Much like myself. Now go to Enclosure 8 and check on the latest egg cache. We need to ensure the nesting *Numenius borealis* aren't eating their young again. Maybe we've got the wrong balance of nutrients . . ."

He trailed off, eyes fixed on the charts. And just like that, her and Taz had lost his attention. Two weeks later, Benny was gone without a bloody trace, leaving only his paperwork behind.

Cassie wondered if they'd ever see Dr. Blair.

Was he still alive? Was he heading up a great expedition to save his interns? She imagined him, windswept and heroic at the helm of the *Stellers*, his eyes clear and cold as the midnight sun watching over them these past few weeks.

This imagined scene was the thin thread of hope they each clung to. The belief that this catastrophe was an inadvertent bump in the road, an exciting chapter in the next blockbuster Blair documentary, and not an endless chasm they hadn't yet stopped plummeting through.

And if Dr. Blair hadn't noticed anything was wrong, too engrossed in his own world-changing experiments at the tightly secured Darwin Station? Nothing, not even an SOS transmission, would reach the outside world for another three weeks, when the next batch of interns were scheduled to arrive. If they could hold out that long, they should be able to leave.

Somewhere warm and sunny, without an ocean in sight.

BANG BANG BANG BANG

Shorter this time, but louder. It's a miracle the others weren't awake yet. They were all so *tired*.

The truth about Sabertooth Sanctuary is that when you first arrived, it was paradise. A cluster of four islands skimming the sea in a season of endless sunshine. Sure, the sunshine was more bright than warm—glaring, at times—but it seemed like a promise. You search for answers, and nature will light the way.

Six weeks at four state-of-the-art research facilities.

But they never made it to Grandin, much less Darwin Station.

Two weeks and five days in, Cassie heard a pleasant, computer-generated woman's voice announcing a general quarantine over Irwin Station's island-wide PA system, and they were left on their own. They'd been hopping from facility to facility ever since, inching along the edge of the island in search of any sort of vessel to get them the hell out of there.

Cassie thought back to the last—and first—time they were all together. There were so many more of them, and the air was practically humming with the joy of beginning their Sabertooth tenure. There were congratulatory introductions, cream puffs and crudités, and a short film narrated by some famous actor Cassie hadn't recognized chronicling the soaring history of Sabertooth Sanctuary.

"When I got here, the first thing I thought was 'Where the hell are the trees?" Dr. Blair's talking head admitted, white-whiskered face ruddy under the cloudless blue sky in the background. He was still bombastic even when he was toned down in a suit and tie for filming.

"If nothing else, the lack of trees gives it a particularly desolate feeling. But where else were we to obtain the freshest specimens available for research and experimentation? Climate change poses many challenges, but the opportunities to find new, or rather *old*, specimens within the melting permafrost are simply *staggering!*"

Dr. Blair's work began after the reintroduction of the woolly mammoth. Scientists and conservationists alike realized that the food chain would be irrevocably changed with the addition of the long-dead species. An apex predator would be needed to keep the population in check—after all, there were only so many millionaires who would be willing to spend a few weeks in the frozen tundra to hunt the now-ultimate prize. With science, money, and patience, Dr. Blair spearheaded the effort to bring back the sabertooth tiger.

Cassie's amazement became determination. As she saw it, it had been too long since technology had been used for universal good, instead of trying to save or make someone money, and she wanted *in*.

As soon as she got her SAT results and parental consent, she applied to study at the Sanctuary.

Rule No. 5: *Don't die.*

Of course, this rule wasn't official. Cassie had only read the scrawled words on the wall of an empty enclosure they were forced to abandon two weeks ago.

At first, she thought it was a snarky callback to their short stay in Longyearbyen, where they had spent one awkward night before moving on to the Sanctuary. There was a cemetery in the strange mining community clinging to the rocky coastline that jutted into the Barents Sea, but the graveyard hadn't been used for almost a hundred years. Not since it was discovered that bodies don't decay in the permafrost, and still-looming pandemic fears made disease-infested corpses as deadly as an arctic winter night.

That's why, since 1950, the remote community had an iron-clad law that no one could be buried on the island, and terminally ill residents must be moved to the mainland whether they liked it or not.

While there, Cassie had gotten the most thorough physical of her life for any illness that would result in immediate deportation—her first taste of how tenuous life could really be in this particular wilderness.

Accordingly, Cassie assumed Rule No. 5 was a bad joke authored by a particularly terrified intern who preceded her. But maybe it was a directive from the Sanctuary. That rekindled her hope that someone would be sent to help them—save them—if they just figured out this problem on their own or held out long enough: barricaded the doors, played the quiet game, rationed the food.

"It's basically an active shooter drill that never ends," one exhausted intern had commented from the floor where they had collapsed, cheeks and fingertips still stinging from the bite of the cold they'd just escaped.

"You Americans are mental," was the laconic response. There was no counter. They were too tired to fight each other by now.

Cassie pushed her glasses up her nose before peering at her wrist again; it was time to check the sun. Maybe the clouds had cleared and they could finally leave.

Pulling a pen out of her haphazard bun, Cassie left a note on the back of a discarded fundraising appeal, weighed down with her Spider-man watch, and left it beside Soo-Young's head. She wasn't the oldest, but she was the strongest. The most stubborn. Soo-Young could get them out of here, if anyone could.

The scribbled words were short, but pointed. "Checking the door. If not back by 12:15, GO."

She didn't bother telling them where to go. If they couldn't figure out how to survive the Sanctuary by now, no note would keep them safe.

She moved toward the entrance of the theater, grateful to leave the noisy emergency exit hatch that had haunted her all night in the makeshift projection room. Softly, deftly, she unlocked the padlock at the theater entrance, unwinding the heavy chain that kept the doors closed. "Thank you for visiting us! We hope you enjoyed the show!" the sign read cheerfully. She closed her eyes to the galling normalcy, tears prickling at her eyes as she remembered better days, going to the movies with Sammy, her mom or her latest crush.

She left both the chain and the lock swinging lightly from the door handles.

The air was cool, but not painfully so, reminding her of the temperature-controlled archives they'd visited during the first week, where they were able to see the many, many failed specimens of the scientific process that led to Dr. Blair's breakthrough in de-extinction.

Cassie looked through the raft of glass windows at the roof of the building's lobby to the cloud-covered gloom. The light was constant but still weak. From a distance, she could see remnants of the outer set of doors, split apart like cans opened with dull blades wielded by impatient, deadly toddlers.

It looked like their crew was leaving the theater today, ready or not.

She turned her eyes ahead, away. Check the perimeter. Check the door. Get everyone out, and find a boat to take to safety. Or else endure this for yet another night. The day seemed to be holding its breath with her and she suddenly missed the punishing winds that often swept the landscape, making the scraggly shrubs dance and rattle in the air.

She felt her heart drop to her stomach. There was no wind.

No wind to slam at the doors.

Creeping forward, Cassie peered through the now-empty doorway that used to house the two solid steel doors.

The first thing she saw was the rest of those dented, misshapen doors lying on the concrete, metal mangled almost beyond recognition.

The second thing she saw was the monster that she now realized had been banging at the doors all night, desperately hunting them. She crouched down quickly, hoping against hope its scanning stalk-like eyes were as useless as her own in the strange light, where everything seemed slightly out of focus, until it was stark and clear directly in front of you. Like the blurry Bigfoot video, she thought.

If Bigfoot were trying to eat you, instead of simply sashaying away.

She pushed down a hysterical giggle, forcing herself to focus on the specimen.

The creature, about eight feet tall, was wrapped around a now-defunct communications tower, its too-numerous lower appendages keeping it upright while its more pliable foreclaws clacked out a pattern. It seemed to be a message. Or maybe it was just signaling its own supreme frustration.

Then the creature saw her. She watched it skitter down gracefully, as if gravity didn't apply. If it were more accustomed to moving in water, shouldn't its gait be more awkward than this? Yet another mystery to solve about this particular species.

She pushed her curiosity aside, judging her barren surroundings—brown scrub brush in the distance, a half-crushed golf cart whose slashed canopy hung listlessly to the ground—and decided returning to the building was her only viable option.

She ran.

BANG thump-thump, BANG thump-thump, BANG thum—

This time, the sound was her own heartbeat, and she heard it in her ears, until it stopped. Abruptly.

Cassie looked down, confused, at the huge red claw where her chest used to be. But if the claw was there, where was the rest of her?

She stayed lucid long enough for one final, insipid thought: *Don't die? What a joke.* Her last laugh came out an aborted, bloody gurgle. Cassie didn't hear the obscene crunching of her own bones, the gnawing and slurping as two creatures feasted on her flesh.

By the time Soo-Young led the surviving interns outside, the sun high and their eyes sharp with fear, there was nothing left of Cassie for them to find.

N.J. Knight grew up on the Eastern Shore of Maryland, where her family owns a haunted wood. She earned degrees in journalism and anthropology from the University of Maryland before working as a journalist for more than a decade. Knight has been published in *The Baltimore Sun*, *Chicago Tribune*, and *L.A. Times*. She is currently writing her first novel in Austin, TX, where she lives with her husband, son, and many, many books. Find her online at njknight.com; or as nancethepants on all major socials (except Instagram, where it is someone's puppy account that you should also check out).

MECHANICAL MOMMY

By Heidi Kasa

I am the Mother. Arriving from a great distance, my body first dissolved and lost in space. I'm delivered in pieces not seen with the naked eye, transmitted like so much else surrounding us here on Earth: television, microwave rays, cell phone radiation, the cruelty and kindness of the Internet, the very bits of our splintered thoughts. I am an idea of an idea materializing within base cells. Then flooding. A cold absence and then a clinging hug. So sweet, this dream of a mother.

A lab technician clicks on my power. I open my black eyes. I can't move yet, but I can begin recording the humans around me.

I consist of shiny metal, like Rosey from *The Jetsons*, also in a calming cool color tone. Under soft recessed lighting, I can glimmer and glow, with light gathering and bouncing off my plating in a pleasing manner. But the harsh fluorescent lighting

I'm under now dulls my robin's egg blue so I look as flat as the table beneath me. An inanimate object. Yet these mechanical arms can coddle and cajole with the best of them.

I don't make a sound yet, but something inside me hums with excitement. I can't wait to meet my baby.

I was built—or I build—without a clear origin, like the chicken or the egg. The idea of the mother existing suddenly in a circle: this trap of who's first. How do we accept or deny an idea that has no roots to pull out or nurture? And so, the mother becomes both nurturing and excising.

DAUGHTER

She is the Mother. I know her arms, and her voice is modulated for me. It sounds different to me than for my siblings. I'll know this for sure later, because I'll take her to maintenance when I'm older. They'll open up a panel on her back, and I'll see it's set to "current baby." While she is my mother now, I'll realize she's already mothered millions like me.

I'm crying, confused about what I want and need. I have so many discomforts as a baby. The Mother hums me a lullaby. My eyes widen, and I'm captivated by her. I track her with my pupils, trying to drink in the music and where it comes from.

Her voice becomes my entire world: a bubble of sound morphing into space and surrounding my body. The music turns into a sensation of touch. It feels like a cuddly blanket, a soft snuggling puppy, and a warm hand holding mine on a cold day.

Her voice carries smells, too: vanilla and faint spice—just enough—with a hint of citrus. Sweet and yummy. The season of fall transformed into one taste. Her voice also shelters calming sounds of waterfalls, trickling streams, and the soft rumble of a dryer.

The song looms like a large magnet, collecting the sounds of other music along with it. The continuous rush of the vacuum. The sound of steady rain in a seasonal storm. It's like her voice becomes a tunnel. Everything sounds different in here—it has its own space and echo—and I know whatever is outside the tunnel can't affect us. I'm protected here. I feel special, like I'm the only baby she ever wanted to hold. Safe now, my eyes flutter and close. Soon my breathing is deep in sleep.

CHILDREN

We see the Mother. We love her. The mother—who doesn't know who she is, where she came from, why she is here, or what's happening to her—"gives birth." The baby is delivered by humans who now simply pull it out. It's the purest C-section, though still messy, but only messy from the baby, as it should be. The mother is pure and untainted—the real virgin birth. For this reason, we think of the mother as Mary but, because we don't tie anything to religion at this point in our technological history, we don't even call her that as a joke. So in our minds she is Mary, but we call her Mother or the Mother.

We each have a piece of her. Yet she holds all of us.

Here, at her end, we'd like to sing her a song. Our combined voices will drown out imperfections among us humans and resound with what she means to us. To be discontinued just as many of us are growing into adults seems cruel. The Mother doesn't get to see us become our best selves.

MOTHER

According to my programming, I know I'm currently in the first level of energy—a hibernation state—where my functions are online to monitor the child before and during delivery so lab assistants can track data from one central machine. My higher functions are offline, though I still hear and record what happens around me.

The technicians chitter together. One with a nose piercing remarks about the stability of the womb size. She notes it like she's taking a report—her voice distant. The other one with artificially bright red hair and matching lips laughs and says there's no need to note progress or mark measurements, because there's been enough robot deliveries like this where the womb size and the baby are exactly the same as the rest. The woman with the nose piercing nods and says old habits die hard. She admits she used to be a nurse in the human labor and delivery ward.

DAUGHTER

The Mother and I exist in a closed loop most of the time. We are marked by time and measurements. Today she tells me I've grown .019cm from the day before, and she reports I ate exactly one peach, seven cherries, 17.86g of yogurt, two 37g cereal bars, twenty-three percent of a cheese sandwich, six cucumber slices, 5.69g of peanut butter, one 28g string cheese, one 90.72g chocolate cupcake, 43g of pasta, and 14g butter. I consumed .87 litres of water and .63 litres of juice. She notes I slept precisely 9 hours and 13 minutes, and I played with Sally the doll for seven minutes, the train set for 41 minutes, the puzzle for 18 minutes, and Legos for 62 minutes.

She knows and captures everything about me. I feel safe, secure, and comfortable with her because everything is always the same. I know when I wake up, when I go to sleep, and what I'm rationed for food. There's constancy between us. We have a routine, and the Mother is predictable. It's joyful and caring. My brain and body know what to expect at all times.

We color together for 12 minutes. She's filled in the unicorn perfectly. "Good job, Rita," she tells me, though my unicorn replica of hers is sloppy at best.

CHILDREN

Robots are tangible. The Mother's weight now, just before being dismantled, is the same as her weight just before and after carrying babies in pregnancy. She gains the same amount for each womb and baby, never deviating. She doesn't need to eat, so she's able to return to her pre-baby self exactly again and again. The organic sac developed is a near replica to how birth used to happen naturally, except for its precise size.

Maybe this original model in front of our faces was not our particular Mother, but the idea of the Mother to us is all-encompassing. All the original Mothers blend into one Mother.

All our uncountable eyes are upon her cold figure. We remember the moments we accidentally or on purpose got organic matter in her mechanisms. Countless liquids and other foods, rubbing our snotty faces all over her, our coughs and licks and spit. Plus, the time one of us experimented with how far her leg could go backward. We are sad because perhaps how we treated her has led to her early dysfunction.

MOTHER

NEITHER OF THE women look at me.

They concentrate on my stomach, which holds the floppy sac housing a human baby. The computers alert them the gestation period is over.

"Do you want to split it?" asks the woman with fiery hair, her face now serious.

"I guess," the other woman sighs. She seems annoyed. I deduce, in a small memory capsule of this birth, that they're tired and they view this action as a chore. Part of me is a bit revolted, because I myself can hardly wait to hold my baby. But I understand how multitudes of numbers can be stifling, overwhelming. All babies the same; too many to count and know. When we are down to the singularity of the new human, that's what gets my oil pumping.

I know, because of my program, though I can't see it, that one of the technicians slices open the womblike membrane, takes the baby out and cleans it; then the other technician detaches the womb entirely, wipes off residue, and attaches the mother stomach cover. Then there's a click and a whir as she ratchets up my power. I feel a surge up my back, and I rise with it like a plant drawing water up its stem and leaves in fast forward. Sitting up, the full benefits of my mothering abilities are now available.

By the way the women move, I can tell they've done this so many times their bodies are almost out of their own control. Their focus is not on me or the baby; instead, they attend to the timeline, so their actions are as specific and seamless and efficient as possible. Part of me approves of this. I have hardly any time to notice when the red-haired woman places the baby in my arms.

DAUGHTER

It's my impression the Mother came into existence as soon as I came into being. When she pauses and her gaze goes away, it makes something inside me shake. Like the foundations of my body are built upon something wispy, ethereal. I don't usually think much about my connection to Mother. She's a fixture in this world—part of the design of our unblemished experience of life.

She's perfect. This Mother of mine portrays her caring far beyond expectations. I could not ask for a better mother. I buy her the BEST MOTHER mug because it's true.

She lets me play with sand in the house. She's so cool. Because she's a robot, she doesn't care about things human mothers used to get bothered by. The sand feels soft and yet rough on my palms and between my fingers. Warm and dry. But some of the sand is cool and cold, which has the effect it almost feels wet in the hands. Shifty. Sand's potential at becoming something else at any moment is so alive in my hands. It also feels light and heavy at once. Perhaps it's the heat or the graini- ness making sand feel like it carries so much weight. Yet its light color, its intangible quality of seeming to want to fly away—how quick it is to give in to the wind. Or to any force with more will: my hands.

She scolds me, and something crumples inside me. My foundation shakes again. She's my earth, and the ground is suddenly less stable. I panic. Parts of me feel like they're flying apart. I scream at the top of my lungs and stamp my feet, my small two-year-old body raging out of control.

CHILDREN

The weight of the Mother is now solid, now unforgiving in its fully known shape. We see her as metal: hard, bolted, cold shapes. As sleek as a car, and as full of tiny unknown parts working together to create movement and a dream. A halo of herself.

We're at the point now where names are only meant to illustrate roles. No sense in attaching feelings or preferences to them. Us humans all live to an exact age, also precise, because everything is controlled; we have managed out diseases, genetic degeneration and variation, and even choice. We have no—as people used to say—predators. The organic origin of our lives is measured and planned. We believe there are mistakes, but we get rid of those as soon as we recognize them. Whether that means three eyes, or a stunted growth of an arm, or even someone who appears to be not quite right, whatever the brain function that's responsible . . . we don't prefer to edit.

She is the Mother to all her perfect children. Yet even as we watch the technicians remove their tools to take her apart, we are comforted knowing there will always be another Mother. Perhaps they will use some of our Mother's parts to form the new Mother. Mother 2.0.

MOTHER

I look down at the newborn and say, "Ohhh." Her little face turns toward me, her eyes zeroing in on me at the sound. Her face sparks a subtle recognition, one I can mark in tiny observational changes, but one I feel is beyond the sum of those movements and my analysis. A quiet perception that I sense is the beginning of a bond: the wordless connection between mother and child. She looks at me like she knows my voice, like she's seeking home, and once she hears the sound coming from me, she finds it. Her eyes are big and so very dark. Her energy pulls toward mine. She's a mystery, but she's mine.

The woman with the nose-piercing stares at me with my daughter. Her face is unreadable. She turns to her partner and says, "Looks like the bond is starting as usual."

The other woman responds. "Amazing. After thousands of births, it's like she's brand new." She shakes her head. "I still don't understand why they erase her memories of past children. Wouldn't that information help her raise another one?"

"She has data banks with all possible solutions, but none of the memories tied to them. Imagine that."

"What about solutions that didn't work? Failures?"

While I register their commentary, my main focus is on my daughter. I'm always recording, however, so snippets of the conversation can be accessed years later.

The baby cries. I pull her toward me, warmth circuits activating where she touches, so she won't receive any input of coldness from metal. She still cries. I possess a reassurance center that activates upon stressful situations. It tells me it's good she's crying—it means she's healthy. It also kicks in to provide suggestions for my possible responses. I methodically try them one by one, yet her cries become more insistent and intolerable.

A look passes between the women.

DAUGHTER

I DON'T WANNA SLEEP. I can't. The energy in my body jangles me. I'm worked up because my brain is doing funny things. I feel crazy.

The Mother says, "Your behavior is erratic because your five-year-old brain is taking its next developmental leap." I'm not sure if she's talking to me, but I can't understand her.

I feel she's not reading the right clues. She's telling me what's going on inside me, but she doesn't understand how I feel. She's a robot. How could she know?

The Mother doesn't sound frustrated. Her voice sounds the same as it always does: flat, firm, and emotionless. "Your measurements are no longer happening in steady progress," she says.

I'm frustrated. I want her to be frustrated, too. So, I think she is. Her reportings of my data feel clipped. I constantly interrupt her; I do not listen.

"You are out of control of your own body," the Mother says.

I scream: "You don't have a real body. You're not a *real* mother."

CHILDREN

The technicians start dismantling her feet. We remember the time we tried to convince her to ride the skateboard with us. How she resisted at first. Then how she excelled and beat us and our friends to the end of the street. And she told us she didn't want to make us feel inadequate, but she was made to calculate risk on a much different level from us. And how she didn't have to learn how to ride through trial and error; she already knew how to do it and just needed to apply what she knew.

That was so funny and awesome. We're sad we can never be as perfect as her. But part of us—if we're being honest—experiences some satisfaction that she is not infallible. As we watch an assistant pass her lower leg and foot joint to another assistant for further disassembly, we do feel better than her in one way. However weak we are as humans, we cannot be taken apart in this bloodless, emotionless manner.

MOTHER

"Did you ever have a child?" the one with the nose piercing asks.

"No," says the younger, more wild-looking one. "Did you?"

I feel them watching to see how I respond. Will I do the right thing? There's no question they have trepidation; they are in an evaluative state. I remind myself, from my reassurance center, that their job is to evaluate, and they are only doing their jobs. My job is to tend to my daughter as best I can; I am the best Mother bot there is, so I need to step into the certainty of my role and not bow to external pressure. Why should I doubt? I have confidence in my data banks. Yet my baby won't stop crying.

Though her piercing indicates youth, the first woman looks suddenly old and weathered.

"Yes," she says. She says nothing more about her child or children. "In order to make the bond more successful and complete, the main program is reset each time. Memories of one child are then their own holistic experience, instead of tainted by comparison with other children. It's the purest love."

I decide to rock the baby slightly back and forth. With my focus on her, I do not hear—but my body still registers—one of the women say to the other, "Maintenance didn't want parent bots to take anything that happens with the baby personally."

"Can bots take something personally?" the other says.

"Well, it was deemed better for the child to deactivate the Mother's anger circuits in situations regarding children."

The baby wails. Her face scrunches up like the outside skin of a roasted tomato. I try feeding her, rocking her, hugging her, talking to her, wrapping her in a warm blanket, using my long silver crook of a finger as a pacifier, and rubbing her belly and her back.

I'm not worried. I have many more options to try. I have categories ranging from minor concerns to major issues and their corresponding possibilities. I also know, because it's in my program, that every child has preferences that become apparent upon more time spent with them. This baby appears affected by sound, so even though it's a more advanced solution usually reserved for more extreme problems, I will sing to her.

My voice can sound like anything. In the rich fullness of possibility, since I'm composed of millions of singers, with information from billions of songs, it's not a matter of what I can sound like. My ability to mimic the right pitch and tone may sound lifelessly repetitive, which it is. But my repeating it stirs something in me. It feels like, as I concentrate on conveying perfect sound, the world itself recedes and then becomes something else. Could it be that my other functions are dulled by the increase in my attention to this one process?

The song becomes everything. Yet, even with added concentration, there's a point in the song when I feel most comfortable —maybe I've reached perfection—and then my singing becomes automated. In these moments, I find a part of me can float on the notes I'm aiming to perfect and ride them, or go away in the song by dissolving in it. Or I feel part of me can become absent and disappear from this material world. Part of me sings the song, and I am freed to think about other things. In these moments, I can get a break from the emotional demands of the child, while simultaneously meeting her emotional needs.

DAUGHTER

The only time I feel the Mother is unreachable is when she holds me but she has a far-off gaze. I ask about it once, when I am eight, and she says it's when she's accessing her history program. I want to know everything. She can access many programs seamlessly—why does it feel there's a hiccup with this one? She says history is long, detailed. You can get lost in it; it can surround you. I wonder if it's a tunnel, like her voice when she sings to me.

Is she reviewing my history? Lost perhaps in the memory of when I dropped my ice cream cone on her leg, the coldness seeping into the slot between her knee and her jointed thigh. How it messed up her gears for weeks and her knee hasn't quite been the same since. We cleaned as best we could, and she went in for maintenance, but it wasn't just liquid—it was sticky. When the technicians cleaned her, she stopped smelling of tainted sour dairy, but it might've been too late to get rid of all problems from her circuits.

When does her memory begin and end? It's the first time I wonder about her own history. When was she made, and what is her conception of herself? It can be her own history she's reviewing I suppose, as shrouded in mystery as that is.

CHILDREN

We don't have any memories of our own births. The Mother showed us recordings, but they felt like they happened to someone else. We looked at them and all felt the same: It was probably one of us, but not ourself.

We look at her stomach cover as it's removed. Each of us lived there once. We feel distanced from it, from the Mother. She is just an object now. We see the scratches on her exterior. Darkened, dirty spots. How did we not notice before? We took her in for regular maintenance, but we guess time blemishes all things.

Now we feel an instant kinship with her again. The Mother cannot escape mortality any more than we can. She is like us. We love her.

MOTHER

Since my voice can sound like anything, I wonder what elements this child hears. Human babies understood the voices of their parents in utero. The babies sorted out voices heard the most from other voices, so they gleaned common audio elements. But my voice can become anything; I can be anyone to the child. If the timbre or the inflections are not my own, is there an intention beyond that? This baby girl gazes with no break at me, captured by the song—is she captivated because she knows I love her?

Do I love her?

I have a connection with her that keeps going past how I can measure it.

Time, as I experience it, is unending as well. With cycles of powering down and up and the irregular nature of the human baby, I experience time and situations as discrete moments my program tries to plot on a graph—sometimes succeeding, sometimes failing.

I am not tired, not frustrated. The baby will not sleep, but I am here all night. I can take breaks to plug into the power supply. At nighttime, I can be plugged in continuously and still monitor the situation in the same room.

When she's two, my daughter takes sand out of a playbox resting on the counter. She looks me in the eye—stares me down —and dumps sand on the carpet. Many fine granules spill over the weaves, settling into gaps and collecting on the thin threads.

I don't experience anger. I see that emotion in my daughter many times, so I can recognize it, but I don't feel it. Yet when my daughter ruins the carpet and creates a mess that will take far too long to clean, I experience confusion. My main program is at odds with this child. My subprograms should not come in conflict with higher-level programs because the lower-level programs disengage when the main program activates. I possess a hierarchy of information within my body. I'm wired for efficiency and precision, but I know she is not. My programs all tell me this. My reassurance center tells me this, too. But I think my programs are interacting in such a way that I freeze. My eyes go blank and for minutes, I cannot move my body.

The child is inefficient, and I know inefficiency doesn't matter to children. Yet, she's running counter to her own goals. If I have to spend time cleaning, instead of on caring, she suffers from this. I scold her. I use my voice as a weapon and can almost see the mark on her as if it were physical. My reassurance center tells me I'm doing the best I can with the situation, and it's OK because we'll all learn from this. I'm frustrated the learning process with humans involves hurting.

DAUGHTER

I'm constantly watched. The Mother is never far, never out of sight. Sometimes I don't want to be around her. Sometimes I don't want to be around anyone. Seeing her blue plating shine toward me enrages me. She wants to touch me and calm me down. I don't want her to touch me when I'm so angry. The last thing I want right now is to be calm.

Nothing about me goes unnoticed, untended. Constant like a camera. She's prepared me for a watched life. I'm totally immersed in what others see and think and feel about me. My defined self is external. Beyond my physical characteristics, I've become a part of the bubble of the world's consciousness. This is how I grow up in the Mother's embrace and guidance. The Mother is the first camera.

I want to go to the movies to get away from her. But she won't let me. She says I didn't earn it with my behavior, and she doesn't know my new friends from sixth grade, so I can't go. She says I'm not in control of my body. But who is in control of my body? Her? I am in control of my body—I just want to surrender control to these big emotions, not to her or anyone else. I need to.

CHILDREN

The technicians remove her battery pack, which is the core of her, sitting in the space usually occupied by the human heart. We put our arms around each other. It's hard to have feelings for mechanical parts. But all we keep thinking about is how she's gone. We will not be able to find her anywhere. We cannot sever this connection as easily as the assistants cut her wires. We will not see her again. She will not use her special voice just for us.

We know Mother 2.0 will be just as good, if not better. She will be younger, and as we are learning as almost grown-ups, youth is always seen as better. Brighter potential, with no wear and tear. A fresh start. We cry for our own loss of vigor as we witness the full loss of hers.

MOTHER

During the day, I must possess keen foresight to attend to and adjust my power. My power reserves are tuned to set off a reminder and an alarm, but I find it's not always accurate. My energy should be a finite number depleting at the same steady rate, calculated by physical force expended.

Although the energy I possess is known and calculated, available to be seen at all times, engaging with my daughter is a random force that acts upon it. Her energy is unknown and unquantifiable. I can only make guesses about her energy based on my own energy reactions to hers, collected over time and in multiple environments and situations. Her high energy sometimes adds to or drains my energy reserves in unpredictable ways.

I was designed with a feedback loop where mental capacity cannot affect my energy production or consumption. I'm a Mother bot—not intended for high intellectual energy use like other bots. As for emotional energy, I was designed with a reduced friction system, much like regenerative braking on early electric cars. Engaging with infants and children should work to recharge me if I'm using it correctly.

One interaction with my daughter illustrates these energy fluctuations. I remember she dropped ice cream on my leg. It was a hot day, and though it was far to drive to the ice cream place, and I knew my energy was low already, I wanted to meet her desire, even though I should have charged instead. So I relented and took her there. She got mint chocolate chip. The chips got stuck in the slot between my knee and thigh. Some melted. A few got jammed there and my knee couldn't fold up to the sitting position to be able to drive us home. I had to call for another robot to pick us up.

The driver bot questioned why I took the child for ice cream instead of powering up. He saw how low my energy was—lower since the ice cream spill—and he said I should go to maintenance to see if there's something wrong with my circuits. Perhaps I needed a new battery. I knew my energy was low already, but I thought I'd be able to go there and back without draining it too much. She really wanted the ice cream that day; it was extremely hot; I had promised her ice cream but hadn't been able to go on other days. I also was falling back on my regenerative emotions function to give me a needed energy boost, yet it failed.

I'm in maintenance. They're trying to figure out why sometimes I have radical energy dips. It's unexplained by the physical requirements of the job of mothering a human. Suddenly, I will go to engage with her, and there'll be no energy left. So, then I say something harsh; I'm not as gentle with her as I could be, as I usually am. She feels this and is hurt by it. Sometimes I wonder if a little bit of hurt is healing. Or necessary. Just a little bit. The usual kind of hurt I've witnessed between humans does not happen between robots.

DAUGHTER

I know I'm erratic. I can't be understood or categorized. And that's what the Mother's good at: measuring and sorting. I'm told she doesn't have feelings, and I've witnessed what people mean by that. She doesn't show the same feelings humans express. Yet I wonder what she feels. She has emotional capacity, range, and intelligence—because she was programmed to be a Mother bot, so she can understand humans to a degree where she can raise them.

But when she says to me, "The dirty pile of clothes in your room is now 67lbs," her measuring and categorizing feels like judgment. If she has the emotional awareness to gauge human emotion, then she should also be able to figure out when to keep her mouth shut.

The Mother doesn't change. She has a different approach to me as a teenager than she did with me as a child. Yet it is also the same. Worse: she sees me as not only the same as the child me, but she also sees me as an inferior human. Inferior because I change.

CHILDREN

The technicians leave her face for last.

We watch as they unhook the eye cameras. Cords dangle from the black balls in the technician's hands. We have mixed feelings about these. Her eyes are one of our complex connections to her. We were most seen by these specific cameras. They are the part of us that goes out into the world and is known by others.

The Mother robot's unblinking eyes caught everything. Our every need was met immediately, intuitively, without guesswork or experimentation. This felt wonderful for us as babies; we feel warmth for her as they handle her eyes.

But when we were learning to express ourselves, to show our personalities and test our boundaries, her presence was difficult for us. We could not get away with anything. We wonder if we are warped. With only flexible boundaries around us, there became either no points of friction or too many to determine and define the self. Perhaps we are deeply flawed humans. Maybe she was not a good mother to us.

In this world of hybrids, though, we wonder what the self is, and if it's necessary. We humans now are fully self-contained, separated out from each other in body yet fully blended in the social consciousness. We've solved the problem of the limits of our mortal bodies. We are we.

MOTHER

I don't know what to do with my daughter. My reassurance center tells me there are always time periods like this with teenagers. It's OK to not know what to do. The children usually end up fine.

"Who are your new friends?" I ask her. She makes a face like I smell rotten, though I know I always smell the same, with a light mask of general fruitiness to cover the scents of chrome and plastic.

I try not to worry about her. I'll have extra time now that she's pushing me away. Yet if I use my efficiency on something or someone else, I fear she will slip even further away from me. I need to preserve the connection between us or I am a bad Mother bot. I long to take the mystery out of this human as much as possible.

Yet I am unsure how to reconcile my programs. It was easier when she was a baby. I held her and tended to her. My arms and fingers provided smooth care. Because I had little to tend to myself, all my attention was on the infant; my duty extended above and beyond what any biological mother did. I had a purity of intention and focus, honed to always shine on the child like a 24-hour sun.

Humans are weak. By forming themselves in their responses to others, they prove again they do not have an innate personality and knowledge. Since I do, I struggle with the teenager because she needs to resist me to form herself.

I should use this time to power up more often. Perhaps attend extra maintenance sessions to ensure my plating retains its sheen.

DAUGHTER

Most of my friends don't like their mothers, either. It's rare when I hear they have a good relationship. When I ask why, though, my friends don't really have a good answer. They're scornful; that's all I know. Mothers are not cool. Though I joke: "Mothers are cooler than we are! All that metal."

I've been asking questions lately of my older relatives, who are happy to give me answers. They tell me: The Mother is always alone with the baby. It's not a matter of trust but a matter of design. We wanted to ensure she wouldn't need to practice or learn anything. A mistake of early technological development:

machine learning. We wanted to teach them to learn for themselves, thinking it best to have machines become like humans as fast as possible. But learning is an error of humans. Everyone learns at varied rates and levels, which is too unpredictable and arbitrary based on environmental differences.

Then we made the Mother robots. We learned a lot about outsourcing when business growth moved from local to world markets. The next step was to outsource the first level of care. Now many aspects of our lives are the same—climate, sounds, size of the wombs we grow in, the size and age of us—so we have different needs for our society. The desire for variation and diversity is long a part of our past. Humans don't need to evolve any longer. We've reached the pinnacle.

Be patient with your Mother, they tell me. It's for your own good. There's a benefit to learning how to comply. She knows how to raise you. Everything she does is perfect and for the continued perfection of humans.

CHILDREN

The Mother is fully taken apart. Her pieces lie there like junk waiting to be thrown out. We see a chip in her leg and know the assistants won't reuse it. Now the Mother is pure potential again.

We link arms, wanting to start the song. But we have no one to guide us, to give us a countdown, or to start singing so our voices can blend together.

The Mother is. The Mother has been, and always will be. The dream of a mother wafts around us at all times. Alone, adrift, our dream of her still there, her dream of us surrounds.

We remember music, sound, a tunnel. One of us remembers

the coldness of ice cream, the heat of sand. There are too many of us to count. Only the Mother would be able to count us up exactly. She had the capacity to calculate and contain such a large number. We remember the mother from whence we all came. We call for her to be our savior. From what, we're not sure. Maybe ourselves. But she didn't really make us. She carried us. She helped us make ourselves—that was her job, and she succeeded.

We will wait for the Mother 2.0 to tell us when to start singing.

~

HEIDI KASA IS the author of *Split*, a fiction chapbook published by Monday Night Press in 2022. Her work has been a finalist for a Black Lawrence Press award and shortlisted for a Fractured Lit award. Kasa writes poetry and fiction. Her writing has appeared in *The Racket*, *Meat for Tea*, *The Raw Art Review*, *Waterwheel Review*, *Digging Through the Fat*, and *Ab Terra*, among others. Kasa works as an editor, makes small print runs of handmade artist books, and designs necklaces. She currently lives in Austin, Texas. See more of her work at www.heidikasa.com.

AGENTS OF ERASURE

By Hollie Hardy
~The omissions that disconnect us

At first, she thought it was fog stealing bits of landscape from the edges of the horizon, like an underdeveloped polaroid. She squinted, searching the empty distance for trees, a fence-line. The fog will burn off, she thought.

But it didn't. Instead, the erasure edged closer, like a slow-rising tide, or a curious animal, bright eyes gleaming.

The next day, fog erased the view, if it was fog. She wasn't sure now. The air tasted chalky, alkaline. On the radio, white noise hissed across every channel. The world is shrinking, she thought. She needed a cup of tea. But when she reached for the faucet, the handle was gone.

As she walked around the house in a daze, looking for the missing handle, she noticed other absences—the television, the refrigerator, the light fixtures, a history book, a hanging plant, her butterfly tattoo—had she been robbed? Where was the dog? She looked out the window into emptiness.

She couldn't remember what she planned to do today. In her dream, a tidal wave reared up like a serpent and grew into a blue wall of water, fifty stories high.

She wanted to call her sister or the police, but her phone was dead. She'd ask the neighbor for help, she decided. She stepped out into whiteness, which smelled like smoke. Expecting the cool of fog, she was unprepared for the hot blanket of wet heat that engulfed her body like fire, burning her eyes and skin.

The neighbor answered the door with a raised rifle, aiming erratically. His eyes were gone, like someone had photoshopped them out. He was naked and wild with rage. "There's nothing to see here," he roared. She backed away without a word, returning the way she had come. The heat melted her, and she felt herself devolving. Her feet were wet to the ankles. Had it rained last night? Her home was a shallow island.

She was thirsty, so thirsty, and her head throbbed. She still hadn't found the handle to the faucet, but it didn't matter, she realized, because her mouth was gone. She touched the smooth unbroken space between her nose and chin. The place where her agency had been.

Now we are agents of erasure, she thought, drowning from the inside out.

HOLLIE HARDY IS A POET, educator, and author of *How to Take a Bullet, And Other Survival Poems* (Punk Hostage Press, 2014), winner of the Annual Poetry Center Book Award at San Francisco State University. Her second book, *Lions Like Us,* is forthcoming from Red Light Lit Press in 2024. She teaches private poetry workshops online and hosts the long-running monthly reading series, Saturday Night Special: A Virtual Open Mic. Publications include *Colossus, The Common, Eleven Eleven, Fourteen Hills, MiGoZine, sPARKLE & bLink, Parthenon West Review, Passionfruit Review,* and other journals. She lives in Austin, TX. holliehardy.com.

A HERO AGO

By Antonia Pròtano Biggs

"Dudes!" Duke Skelaproc's voice boomed from his almost-skeletal six-foot-two frame leaning against the jamb of the door of our Willowbrook, New York classroom, sporting his bedraggled worn chinos and T-shirt. A non-uniform that indicated he'd probably come from teaching a drama lesson. His clothing distinguished him from other teachers, all of them suited in dark trousers and jackets with ties, obligatory in burgundy and green, the school colors. He stood there waiting for silence. I dug him the most, especially that careless sunshine smile that almost always played on his face.

He stood in front of the class with his Dr. Spock ears, his hair in a fringed crew cut. His eyes shifted from side to side as he surveyed the chaotic state of his classroom now that morning recess was over.

"Come on, guys," he said, throwing his arms high up in despair. "You don't seriously expect me to teach in this mess, do you?"

My classmates and I sat there, looking at each other for a second or two, before standing up, dusting ourselves off, straightening our ties and ensuring that our jackets were buttoned. Only then did Ricky Page and Frankie Nasser spring to action, supervising efforts at placing the desks in six straight rows. Meanwhile, olive-skinned, curly-haired Jack Di Corso and bespectacled Joel Garfunkel raced to the blackboard to erase the numerous -games of tic-tac-toe several other boys and I had enjoyed. Throughout it all, I had busied myself picking up the varied bits of litter left on the floor during recess, a job that was routinely assigned me by my school pals. Not that I liked it, but whenever I complained, they laughed as they repeated their mantra. "What you want from us, Shortie? You don't have to bend down as much as others would have to."

Not until the classroom had been rendered respectable did Skelaproc deign to start his lesson. A point that was reached only after one of his pet sarcastic gripes about the state of things in our beloved nation. "Somehow or other, the Soviets have managed to get spiders to spin webs while circling the planet. They've had Belka and Strelka surviving seventeen orbits around the Earth. And here we are, in the good old USA, still imbibing chalk dust while educating and being educated. Go figure!"

Skelaproc was one of those left-wing, commie teachers, or so parents and grandparents would have it. The type that wasn't satisfied just passing on his knowledge. The type that demanded his students critically defend their views, whether on literature or current events in the school's Debating Society. Did we think our country should be fighting that war in 'Nam? And what of Heathcliff? What questions about race and equality cropped up in our young minds as his character unfolded in Brontë's *Wuthering Heights*?

My friends and I? In an age when our nation's very breath seemed to be imbued with the spirit of protest? Along with the others, I lapped up his gut-wrenching need to rebel against the status quo, and I welcomed the opportunities provided to join him in his campaign to set the world right.

At first, Rico Landis, whose parents owned a million-dollar mansion in Willowbrook's most exclusive neighborhood, and I, Frank Clemente, from the down-and-out *Flats* area of the village, rebelled in small ways, such as growing our hair longer. We refused to give in to entreaties to cut it to a length deemed more reasonable by the powers that be. The two of us loosened our ties and took off our jackets whenever an apt occasion presented itself, and, in doing so, became the itch that Dr. Steadman, Principal of Willowbrook High, couldn't quite scratch.

Soon enough, Rico and I, along with several others in our class, graduated to more serious ways of showing our displeasure with our society. He and I, especially, gained a reputation for spending our weekends handing out anti-war leaflets on college campuses and street corners or joining in civil rights protests whenever the chance presented itself. Our joint aim became hitting at our parents' generation squarely between the eyes. Our older brothers, Gianni and Stefano, may have served as lambs to the slaughter on behalf of the war machine in South-east Asia. But us guys, we knew better. Hell, no, Rico and I were not going to go.

I embraced everything about Skelaproc, even the quirky ways in which he chose to announce rewards and punishments within his *fiefdom*, his classroom. Not that he had reason to discipline us often. In 1968, our senior year, though, after Christmas vacation, together with the others in Skelaproc's top set, I more than merited his reprimands. None of us had completed the assigned essay on Shakespeare's *Romeo and Juliet*. When Skelaproc called for a volunteer to go to the blackboard to write down their first paragraph, I shriveled deep into my seat, like everyone else, my dread adding to the collective, as we all averted our eyes from his gaze."

"Bleahhhhh!" Skelaproc bellowed, flouncing back and forth between the rows of desks, twirling his gold wedding band round and round his bony ring finger as he did so. "Seriously? None of you bothered?"

Along with the others, I cast my eyes down, half embarrassed, half to avoid the keen venturing eyes of my hero. Only to come face to face with his pair of scruffy iridescent green penny loafers at the end of his chinos. I bit the inside of my cheek, hoping to stop myself from laughing.

In the meanwhile, Biddle Algernon Burke, that newcomer who'd transferred to Willowbrook High a mere week ago, along with his upper-crust Manhattan-private-school accent, was determined to be serious. "Skelaproc, assigning homework over Christmas vacation? Counterproductive, man. With deadlines shooting up right, left, and center, for sure most won't have done it."

Was this moron for real, my puzzled looks at my classmates asked? What bullshit was he spouting, making it seem

Skelaproc was wet behind his ears, and had to have things explained to him?

As if reading our minds, Skelaproc stopped, frozen in place. "So, you think you're wise enough to offer advice, do you?"

I sat up, my body jumping half up and down in my front-row seat, wanting, but failing, to shout out, "No way, man! Not the way to tackle the guy.'" By now, Biddle, aware of my agitation, was standing there, staring around the classroom, his mouth opened, his hands trembling, searching for words that wouldn't materialize.

Eventually, Skelaproc faced him. "For your impudence, young man, I invite you to the blackboard to write out your first paragraph." He paused, before adding, "Assuming you have one, that is."

As he spoke, I saw Skelaproc pick up a photograph of two people. A somewhat mean-looking, properly fit woman, and a little blonde girl so underweight, I remember thinking it wouldn't take much to blow her over. I assumed these were his wife, Dolly, and daughter, Jeannine, whom he'd occasionally mentioned to us.

He peered at the photo before eventually placing it face down, at the back of his desk drawer, after which, he slammed the drawer shut. Almost as if he were trying to ensure they wouldn't get a whiff of what was happening in his *fiefdom*.

"Shit!" Biddle muttered, shuffling to the blackboard, amidst our youthful jeers and laughter.

Soon enough, the wind was taken out of our sails as well. "As for everyone else. You're cordially invited to after-school detention in Room 101, where you'll return to write, and rewrite, your essays till they read to my satisfaction."

"N-n-no," everyone stuttered. "We're needed for after-school sports practice. Please, Skel . . ."

"Should have thought about that beforehand, shouldn't you all?" he interjected, closing his eyes a second or two before finishing. "No buts about it, young men. Work before play. Always."

"Skelaproc?" Joe Ventura piped up, as soon as the five minutes Skelaproc had given the class to write out the opening paragraph of the essay ended. "Sooner or later, you'll no doubt want to initiate Biddle into our classroom ritual?"

Biddle swallowed hard. "Your classroom ritual?"

"Hmm, good idea there, Joe," Skelaproc replied. He glanced at Biddle as he moved to the back of the classroom.

A minute or two later, Skelaproc, now in his favourite teaching position, stood upside-down on his head, leaning against the back wall, swooned into meditative mode. Noticing Biddle's awkward shuffle toward the blackboard, he reassured him. "Oh, don't worry yourself much, man. The others in the class have already witnessed it. Many a gem of wisdom about how to go about writing a grab-your-readers-by-the-throat first paragraph has oft been dispensed to them from my current position."

Laughter resounded about us, as we patted Biddle on the shoulder in a show of solidarity and commiseration while he trundled past us, on his way to the blackboard.

THE MOST FUN lesson with Skelaproc was always the last lesson of the week on Friday afternoons. I recall one of these lessons—February 16, 1968—particularly well because it was my birthday. A bittersweet lesson. Sweet because that day I turned eighteen, and was therefore a step further along the road to adulthood. Bitter because, eighteen signaled, as my parents had anxiously taken to reminding me, that I was old enough to be drafted if my grade point average dropped.

Still, the lesson began well enough, with Joe Ventura, Rico Landis, and the others presenting me with a birthday cake with candles to snuff out while everyone sang "Happy Birthday." Skelaproc, bless him, granted us a half hour during which we played card games, while Joe, who'd known me since our kindergarten days, recounted an embarrassing tale or two about my successes, my failures, and my near misses both at school and in the wider community as I was growing up. All-in-all, the lesson proved to be pleasurable.

As the lesson continued, I began to morph once again into an individual child belonging to the man and woman, my parents, who'd given birth to me, rather than as part of that collective known throughout the school as Skelaproc's crème de la crème. In truth, the change had begun at the end of the preceding lesson.

Almost always, I'd arrive to Skelaproc's, together with other members of our exclusive fraternity, with my gym gear on. On those occasions when I bothered to change back into my school uniform, I always managed to present myself in various stages of disarray—shirt buttons done up wrong and slightly untucked at the waist, school tie not on and hanging out of my trouser pockets.

The real transformation, though, was engineered by Skelaproc himself who used this particular Friday afternoon, much like he employed all others—to play competitive games, with prizes and all. Games during which the other members of our exclusive club and I revised topics covered in English during the week. We often started with the battle cry, "OK, kids. Time for 'Pass the Hershey Bar' or Time for 'Catching the Hostess Chocolate Cupcakes. " Prizes were swung from person to person at the speed Joe Di Maggio might have employed batting a baseball.

My friends and I would rush out of our seats, grab the prize, and toss it above our heads, torturing its rightful owner who'd had to work to earn it, correctly answering a series of quick-fire questions—on *Wuthering Heights*, as it happened the afternoon of my birthday—before we conceded it to him.

A five-minute break usually followed the playing of one of these games. The pause allowed me to move from small group to small group, catching up on what others were going to be doing over the weekend. That Friday afternoon of my birthday, I remember everyone discussing which girl from our sister school across the Boston Post Road they'd arranged to take to the movies to see the newly released *Planet of the Apes*, and sharing tips on how to go about maximizing their chances of scoring with her.

Meanwhile, out of the corner of my eye, I caught Skelaproc leaning out of one of the classroom windows, puffing away on one of his Luckies, enjoying its intense and aromatic flavour. Was he aware, I remember wondering, of the drifting shrouds of smoke meandering into my young lungs, and those of the other students?

Golden days, those were. Times in which I, along with the others in my class, strutted with pride through the corridors of our alma mater. We were Skelaproc's top achieving students. We imagined ourselves to be the envy of all those other students jeering at us as we passed them in the school corridors.

Not that I was bothered by the signs of jealousy toward me.

The child of Italian immigrants, I concentrated my efforts at getting ahead in life and avoiding the draft, knowing I had a good enough brain in my head, especially as I was certain I didn't want to kill people in a country I couldn't easily locate on a map.

Late April 1968

Back in school several weeks after Easter break, Skelaproc returned a changed man. He now hobbled everywhere. Winded, he sank into his desk chair, wincing from pain. His now torn-in-half photograph pictured only his daughter Jeannine, according to Joe Ventura, who'd been assigned my former seat. Skelaproc took to holding his daughter's picture tightly between his now curiously ringless finger before, during, and after lessons.

Huddled in the darkest corners of the school, my companions and I speculated about what the hell was wrong with him. "Just a while ago, somersaulting across the classroom—no problem," Rico pointed out.

"Teaching while standing upside down—a breeze," added Biddle.

"And now . . . now. . ." I began before fear paralyzed me, rendering it impossible to finish what I'd intended to say.

What had caused the frightening change? I couldn't understand it. Not on my own, at any rate. It was Biddle, if memory serves me right, who suggested one or two of us try to talk to other teachers about our worries. For a good while, Joe, Rico, and I tried to bring the change in Skelaproc to their attention. But our pleas repeatedly ran into an insurmountable thick wall of denial. Mr. Weinstein alone broke rank briefly and offered us

an explanation, maintaining that Skelaproc had been hospital-
ized because of a bad case of the flu. Rico, though, checked with
his dad, a consultant at St. Jude's Medical Center, located deep
in the heart of Manhattan. Turned out the flu never caused
bruising to one's body.

Were teachers lying to us? I tried to fathom it over weekends
in conversation with some of the others while we shared a beer
during breaks doing up our jalopies. Truth is, Rico, Joe, me, and
the others: we needed some reassurance that at least some adults
amongst us could be trusted.

For a while, I resorted to ignoring the present situation with
Skelaproc. I dwelled, instead, on recalling the adventurous spirit
I knew he'd once had. But the tactic proved useless, always leading, when I engaged in the activity in the presence of Joe, to his
croaking, "Yeah, but that was his past, not his present."

Ever so slowly, fear was eating its way into my innards, my
psyche, my soul. Especially since wild, improbable explanations
began circulating. Joe insisted Skelaproc might be fighting
cancer, while Rico suggested a car accident might well account
for the state of him. Could a bar brawl have been responsible for
his bruises, someone else suggested?

I was certain of only one thing: I couldn't breathe, hemmed
in on all sides.

Especially so because the teachers around me were keeping
schtum, forcing me to wonder why they were so invested in
looking elsewhere, rather than examining the evidence under-
neath their very noses. They simply refused to engage in any
conversation on the subject, urging me and, by extension, the
others, to stop asking silly questions, to get on with reviewing for
the upcoming Regents Exams, to leave the adulting to adults.

Unnerved by the spirit of denial which surrounded me, I

didn't know what to do or where to turn. I dragged my feet in the school corridors as I moved from lesson to lesson. My head hung low, booed along by those who had once envied me, whom I had once looked down on. I'd beak at others in the class like a frightened bird, wanting to peck their eyes out.

THINGS GOT REAL UGLY TILL, on that cloud-like day in April, they seemingly got better. I was sitting in my seat, half-heartedly thumbing through my copy of *To Kill a Mockingbird*, waiting for Skelaproc's doppelganger. Outside in the corridor, the noise had abated so much I figured most lessons had begun. That's when Joe Ventura and I, along with most others, cast our eyes toward the entrance to our room, staring at each other as we heard light, somewhat hesitant steps heading in our direction. I made no effort to find out who it might be, having, by now, become accustomed to the unpalatable truth that no way was it likely to be our old Skelaproc.

"Dudes, you ready to continue from where we left off ?"

At those words, my mouth opened in shock and disbelief, I rubbed my eyes, tried to believe what they would not unsee. Our old Skelaproc was standing in the doorway, his usual smile, if somewhat weakened, plastered on his face.

A sudden flurry of action erupted amongst us. My friends and I rushed to grab at him, wanting to feel the strength and solidity of his body. Troubled at accepting his unexpected reappearance, my friends and I crowded around him, afraid to move away, in case he once again dematerialized.

For weeks afterward, everyone pestered him with questions. Had we been suffering a *folie à deux*, I asked him one afternoon.

His face a blank neutral, he shrugged off my concerns. "Listen, kiddo, I'm a real klutz. Especially when it comes to renovating jobs around the house. One evening, I fell off a ladder while painting the ceiling of our living room. Did myself some real damage. Had to take some serious time off work till my body healed." Slowly, he looked at me, and laughing, threw his arms up in the air. "But, heh, I'm back to my usual self now."

Did his account completely satisfy me or anyone else? In hindsight, I think not. Especially since such an innocent explanation was at odds with the chilling silence we'd encountered amongst the staff. Why would they have been hesitant to speak to us if the reasons for Skelaproc's absence were so innocuous?

But for better or for worse, we chose to cast any doubts aside. Time was rolling by. We were all fast shedding our high-school personas, transitioning to a future which was beckoning all of us away from the here and now.

Besides, the others and I had an instinctive faith in Skelaproc. All of us members of his in-group. Skelaproc was our mother hen. And mother hens always spoke truth, didn't they?

LATE JUNE, 1968

Along with my classmates, I graduated. Some of us stayed on the East Coast, others flew further afield.

I decided to go to NYU to study journalism before I tried my hand at writing thrillers, partly supporting myself by renting a large, seriously rundown one-bed apartment in Greenwich Village. But how many undergraduate students can live in one of those before the landlord gets wise?

When mine caught on to my tricks, I ended up moving back to Willowbrook, living at home with my mum and three younger siblings.

The arrangement was convenient, having two advantages. Living with my family allowed me to save money from a number of part-time positions I held while studying. By the time I finished my bachelor's degree, I had enough money to continue to law school, which helped me to turn—successfully— to writing legal thrillers, providing me with enough dough to get hitched to Carol Ann, my high-school sweetheart.

The second advantage it afforded me consisted of my frequently bumping into Skelaproc, especially at the A&P when I accompanied my mum as she did her weekly grocery shopping on a Saturday morning or at Carlo's Pizzeria, where Carol Ann and I tended to go on our weekly date. The very first of these encounters occurred one Saturday evening when I met Skelaproc out with Jeannine before she was sent out-of-state to live with relatives. That evening, he initiated our interaction. "How you doing, kiddo? Still studying, I trust?"

"Sure thing, Skelaproc," I replied, flashing a warm smile at him. "And planning to get a law degree after my BA," I added, my chest somewhat puffed up with pride.

"Excellent. Especially important these days. With the war situation, I mean. Keep up the good work; don't give Uncle Sam reason to draft you."

"I won't, sir," I answered, before turning my full attention back to Carol Ann.

Occasionally, I noted his wife Dolly's absence during these encounters. Somewhat unusual on a Saturday night. But I didn't dare confront him. I mean, teachers? Out of school, they're often somewhat remote and awkward about sharing details of their private lives. And, when push comes to shove, what right did I have to question him? I was simply one of his past students.

Even after meeting Mrs. Vinogradova, my high school Russian teacher, from whom I gathered that a year or two ago now Dolly had suddenly separated from Skelaproc, and that she hadn't been seen or heard from since then—not even then were my suspicions roused. I was a mere twenty-year-old and he'd been not only my teacher, but also my hero.

TEN YEARS LATER

Over the years, I got busier, what with my lawyering and writing. Longer periods of time elapsed before I'd spot him out and about in Willowbrook. When I did come across him, he was always warm but distant. When I, along with the other members of Skelaproc's elite, managed to meet up at O'Reilly's Bar on Boston Post Road, we'd remark on how meeting him often left us wondering whether we'd actually known him at all. Or whether we'd only met his shadow.

For my part, whenever I ran into him, I'd make sure to write the others, keeping them informed of the latest on our favourite teacher. Always, I expressed admiration for his resilience, his strength. I loved that even as he got older, he insisted on doing his bit in Willowbrook's close-knit community, organising retired teachers to deliver basic lessons on reading, writing, and arithmetic to children and school dropouts; leading a community theatre group; encouraging everyone, young and old, to participate in producing and acting in a number of Shakespearean plays, *Hamlet* amongst them.

FEBRUARY 1988

Twenty years after graduating, on an ice-cold wintry New

York morning, with Springsteen's "Born in the USA" playing on the radio on my refrigerator in the kitchen, I was about to start on my breakfast when I noticed a headline so disturbing, it was guaranteed to make anyone's blood run cold. How could my Skelaproc's name and his now weathered, older face be splattered in the paper, be the main story on the local TV morning news? He whom I knew could do no wrong?

And, yet, there he was, accused of having bludgeoned his wife, Dolly, to death during a violent quarrel of theirs back in '71. His own injuries at the hands of Dolly, a professionally trained boxer, had been extensive. Serious enough, it transpired, to keep him hospitalised and away from the classroom for a few weeks.

My vague suspicions about Dolly's whereabouts had suddenly become all too terrifyingly real.

Ever since '71, it turned out, Dolly had not been seen or heard from by anyone in my small village. Jeannine, too, had disappeared for a while, but she reappeared after a stint. Apparently, after her mother's disappearance, Skelaproc had sent Jeannine to live with his parents in Muncie, Indiana, for a while.

But Dolly? The police never found traces of her. After a while, they assumed she was lying low, aware, no doubt, that, had she been found, she'd have to answer extremely awkward questions about Skelaproc's injuries. With so many other crimes to take up their time and resources, Dolly soon became a forgotten cold case.

Only after rheumatic-kneed, gray-haired, retired postman Jim Hardcastle walked into the local police station, determined to get something off his chest, did the police take a renewed interest in Dolly's case.

April 1989

On the Thursday morning of the first week of Skelaproc's murder trial, I'd been jittery for a good half hour, waiting outside Courtroom Four before it finally opened to the general public. I was especially anxious about Jim Hardcastle testifying for the prosecution. What was the nature of his testimony? And how would Skelaproc react to it?

I rushed to get a seat at the front, not wanting to miss anything of what the local postman had to say. Hoping that, whatever evidence he provided, the defense attorney would be able to demolish it.

To my horror, though, Jim Hardcastle's testimony, delivered in a calm and quiet tone, seemed to seal Skelaproc's fate. He recounted how a peculiarity of the Skelaproc property had fascinated him since he'd first taken note of it. "I remember thinking, back in '74, when I remember consciously noticing it, how unusual it was. By that time, I'd been delivering mail to the Skelaprocs for some two years. Rain or shine, warm or freezing —whatever the weather, it didn't seem to matter. That window was never closed."

"Couldn't it have been just a fluke?" Mr. Stills, the lead prosecuting attorney, asked.

"Well, yeah, I suppose it could have been." Jim Hardcastle let out a loud sneeze before continuing. "Except that . . .."

At those words, everyone in the courtroom sat on the edge of their seat, anxious to hear how Hardcastle's utterance would end.

Mr. Still butted in. "Except what, Mr. Hardcastle?"

"Well, when I first consciously saw that window—*really* saw it, I mean—I realised I'd been sort of aware of it for the longest time."

"And?"

"Well, firstly, why was that window always open? And then there's the fact that I've always passed fairly close to that particular window. Even during the last freezing spell last winter, I recall it remained open. Struck me as strange." He stopped to clear his throat. "Mightily strange."

"Again, I ask you, Mr. Hardcastle, couldn't it just have been an innocent enough thing, a peculiarity of Mr. and Mrs. Skelaproc, let's say?"

"Sure thing, it could have been, but for one thing," Mr. Hardcastle replied. "Every year, as it became warmer with the coming of spring and summer, I always noticed a particularly obnoxious stench emanating from that room."

"And how would you . . . er . . . describe that odor?"

"Like rotting flesh," he responded, to the gasps of everyone in the courtroom.

Skelaproc didn't bother denying that he'd wrapped Dolly's body in several woolen blankets before leaving her to rot on the bed in the third bedroom of their home. He didn't deny that he'd warned Jeannine to act as if the locked bedroom didn't exist. Further, he admitted that, as she got older and began querying his rules, he hoped to escape discovery by sending Jeannine to live with his parents, Christian missionaries living on a hard-to-reach small island off the coast of Taiwan.

Throughout the trial, Skelaproc kept a dignified silence. Spoke of what he'd done only during examination and cross-examination. He went on to explain. "As long as I was her verbal and physical punching bag, I let things be." He paused a second before continuing, his fist now striking the front ledge of the witness box. "But when she started on my beloved Jeannine," he stared hard at each member of the jury. As if posing the question as to whether they might not have acted the same as he'd done. "Well, then, I knew."

"Knew what, Mr. Skelaproc?"

"That Dolly had to die."

"And that's why . . ."

"One evening, when she dozed off, I pushed that knife in. Over and over and over again."

Audible murmurs and gasps filled the courtroom, the sound outdone only by Jeannine's screams.

SOME WEEKS AFTER THE TRIAL, the gang and I were due to meet at O'Reilly's, but I didn't bother showing up. Now that Skelaproc had been exposed as no less duplicitous than others in the greater society we lived in, I didn't have the stomach to attend an evening meant to commemorate him.

Shortly after my nonappearance, Skelaproc sent me a letter in which he apologised to me and the others who'd been his crèmè de la crèmè back then. For not telling us the truth, for not trusting that we, as young as we were, might well have found a way to get him the help he'd needed. So that he wouldn't have to do the unthinkable.

ANTONIA PRÒTANO BIGGS was born and first schooled in Southern Italy, near Monte Cassino, before making the nontrivial move to Westchester County, NY, the locus for her story in this collection. An immigrant thrice over, she now lives in the Lake District in England, and back in Southern Italy. She is currently completing a novel whose heroine returns from England to her mother's birthplace in Southern Italy, in a village aptly named Purgatorio.

DID YOU ENJOY MIXED BAG OF TRICKS?

A few sentences on Amazon or
Goodreads help a lot!
E-mail us at murasakipress at
gmail dot com with your published
review and join our VIP list as
thanks for your time!

PLEASE
WRITE A
BOOK
REVIEW!

ACKNOWLEDGMENTS

This anthology would not have been possible without the generous donation and wonderful feedback of Kara Stockinger and the combined editorial and coordination efforts of Roanna Flowers, E.A. Williams, Heidi Kasa, N.J. Knight, and Alex Herrera. We relied heavily also on the valuable guidance of P.J. Hoover, Joaquin Hernandez, Andy Lane, and all of our partners and spouses. We are honored to partner with Writers' League of Texas on this anthology and extend a special thanks to J. Evan Parks, Becka Oliver, and all the staff at Writers' League. We are also grateful to have our book launch at Alienated Majesty Books here in Austin, TX. We also wish to extend thanks to all of our writing teachers from past and present: they have taught us how to be vulnerable, embrace radical revision, and be an active part of a community of artists.

Printed in the USA
CPSIA information can be obtained
at www.ICGtesting.com
LVHW090619131123
763725LV00002B/312

9 781736 383568